The Girl

with the

Golden Eyes

HONORÉ DE BALZAC

The Girl

with the

Golden Eyes

Translated by CAROL COSMAN

CARROLL & GRAF PUBLISHERS, INC.
NEW YORK

Translation copyright © 1998 by Carol Cosman

All rights reserved

First Carroll & Graf edition 1998

Carroll & Graf Publishers, Inc.
19 West 21st Street
New York, NY 10010

Library of Congress Cataloging-in-Publication Data
is available

ISBN: 0-7867-0561-2

Manufactured in the United States of America

The Girl

with the

Golden Eyes

Surely there is no sight more striking than the general aspect of the Parisian population, a dreadful looking people, all yellowish and gaunt. For isn't Paris, after all, a vast field continually awash in a tempest of conflicting interests raging above a crop of men cut down by death more often than elsewhere, always reborn equally harried, exuding through all the pores of their contorted, twisted faces the wit, the desires, the poisons that fill their minds? No, not really faces, but masks: masks of weakness, masks of strength, masks of wretchedness, masks of joy, masks of hypocrisy, all emaciated, all stamped with the indelible signs of a breathless greed. What are they after? Gold or pleasure?

Several observations on the Parisian soul may explain the causes of this cadaverous physiognomy. In

---

This is the third of three stories that constitute the History of the Thirteen—a mysterious secret society—included in Balzac's *Scenes of Parisian Life*.

1

Paris there are only two ages, youth and decay: a bloodless, pallid youth and a decay painted to seem youthful. Seeing these people exhumed, unreflective foreigners experience an initial revulsion for this capital, this vast atelier of sensual pleasures from which soon they, too, are unable to tear themselves away and stay on, becoming willfully deformed. A few words will suffice to explain, physiologically, the almost infernal tint of Parisian faces, for it is not only in jest that Paris has been called an inferno. This word must be taken seriously. Here everything smokes, burns, shimmers, boils, flames, evaporates, gutters, reignites, glitters, glimmers, and consumes itself. In no other country has life been so intense or so stinging. After every completed task this volatile social nature seems to tell itself: "On to the next!" as does nature itself. Like nature, this social nature concerns itself with insects and flowers that live only a day, with trifles and ephemera, and also casts fire and flame from its inextinguishable crater. Perhaps before analyzing the causes of the special physiognomy of each tribe of this intelligent and active nation, we should indicate the general cause that has variously discolored, blemished, paled, and polished its individual members.

The Parisian is interested in everything and, in the end, interested in nothing. Since there is no dominant emotion on his haggard face, it grows gray like the plaster of the houses that have weathered every variety of dust and smoke. Indeed, intoxicated as he is with something new from one day to the next, the Parisian, regardless of age, lives like a child. He complains of everything, tolerates everything, mocks everything, forgets everything, desires everything, tastes everything, feels everything passionately, drops everything casually—his kings, his conquests, his glory, his idol, whether made of bronze or glass— just as he throws down his shoes, his hat, and his fortune. In Paris, no emotion can resist the drift of things, and the struggle to swim against the tide dampens the passions. Here, love is a desire and hatred a whim. There is no real bond of kinship but the thousand-franc note, no friend but the pawnbroker. This general indifference has its consequences; and in the salon, as in the street, no one—whether fool or rogue, decent man or wit—is either superfluous or indispensable, nor is anyone utterly noxious. Everything is tolerated: the government and the guillotine, religion and cholera. You are always welcome in this world, and you are never missed.

What is the dominant force in this land devoid of customs, beliefs or feelings? And where do all feelings, all beliefs and customs begin and end? In gold and pleasure. Use these two words to light your way through this great plaster prison, this hive of black gutters, and follow the twists and turns of the thought that moves it, stirs it, kneads it. Look.

First examine the class that has nothing: The worker, the proletarian, the man who lives by his feet, his hands, his tongue, his back, his good arm, his five fingers. Well, this fellow who should be the first to save his earnings lives beyond his means, tethers his wife to some machine, exploits his child and nails him to a wheel. The manufacturer acts as the string that pulls this people into motion: Their dirty hands fabricate and decorate porcelain, sew suits and dresses, smelt iron, work wood, forge steel, spin and weave hemp, polish bronze, carve crystal, fashion imitation flowers, embroider woolens, train horses, braid harnesses and upholstery binding, work leather, cut copper, paint carriages, pollard old elm trees, spin cotton, dry tulle, cut diamonds, polish metals, carve marble leaves, polish pebbles, groom thought, tint, bleach, and blacken everything. Well, this middleman promises this sweating and eager, industrious and patient people an extravagant wage, either in the name of the city's whims or on the authority of the monster called Speculation. So these four-handed creatures begin working night shifts, suffering, straining, swearing, fasting, hurrying, tripping over themselves in their thirst for that mesmerizing gold. Then, heedless of the future, greedy for pleasure, relying on their strength as a painter relies on his palette, they are lords for a day, throwing away their money on Mondays in the taverns that girdle the city with filth—a girdle of the most indecent daughters of Venus, constantly done up and undone, where this people, as ferocious in their hedonism as they are docile in their work, lose themselves as in a periodic game of chance.

For five days there is no rest for this bustling population of Paris! They surrender to activities that make them twist and swell, grow thin and pale, erupt in a thousand jets of creative effort. Then they take their pleasure and relaxation in an exhausting debauch, which leaves their skin brown with filth, black and blue with violence, blotched with drunkenness, or yellow with indigestion. This lasts only two days but steals tomorrow's bread, the weekly soup, the wife's new dress, and swaddling for the ragged child. These men, who were surely born to be handsome, for every creature has its own beauty, have been disciplined since childhood under the rule of force, under the reign of the hammer, the chisel, the spinning mill, and have been swiftly vulcanized. Vulcan, with his ugliness and strength, is the very emblem of this ugly and powerful nation, superb in its mechanical skill, patient in its time, terrible one day in every century, inflammable as gunpowder, and primed with drink for revolutionary fireworks, indeed intelligent enough to take aim at a captious word interpreted to mean only one thing: gold and pleasure!

If we include all those who hold out their hands for alms, for legitimate wages, or for the five francs allotted to all sorts of Parisian prostitutions, indeed for all well- or ill-gotten gain, this people comprises three hundred thousand individuals. Without the taverns, the government would be overthrown every Tuesday. On Tuesdays, fortunately, this people is numb, sleeping off its pleasure, penniless, and returns to work, to dry bread, prodded by a need for material production which has become habitual. Nonetheless, this race has its pillars of virtue, its unknown Napoleons who typify its strengths carried to their highest expression, and who reflect its social potential in an existence in which thought and action are combined less to maximize joy than to minimize the effects of pain.

Chance may have made some worker thrifty, chance may have graced him with thought; he has been able to look to the future, he has met a woman and become a father; and after several years of harsh privations he starts a little haberdashery business and rents a shop. If neither illness nor vice stops him along the way, if he has prospered, then what follows describes the normal course of such a life.

But first, hats off to this king of the Parisian scene who has submitted to time and space. Yes, hats off to this creature made of saltpeter and gas, who gives children to France during his industrious nights and during the day runs here and there in the service, glory, and pleasure of his fellow citizens. This man resolves the problem of satisfying simultaneously an agreeable wife, his household, the *Constitutionnel*, his office, the National Guard, the Opéra, and God, all for the purpose transforming the *Constitutionnel*, the office, the Opéra, the National Guard, the wife, and God into gold. Indeed, hats off to this peerless workhorse. Up every day at 5:00 A.M., he flies like a bird across the space that separates his residence from Rue Montmartre. In wind or thunder, sleet or snow, he is at the *Constitutionnel* and waits there for the bundles of newspapers he has been commissioned to distribute. He snatches up this political bread and carries it off. At nine o'clock he is back in the bosom of his family, jokes with his wife, gives her a big kiss, drinks a cup of coffee, or scolds his children. At quarter to ten he makes his appearance at the local town hall. There, perched on a chair like a parrot on its pole, kept warm at the city's expense, he sits until four o'clock, registering, without a tear or a smile, the births and deaths of the entire district. The happiness and misery of the district pass through the nib of his pen, just as some hours earlier the wit of the *Constitutionnel* had ridden on his shoulders. Nothing weighs him down! He always goes straight ahead, takes his patriotism ready-made from the newspaper, contradicts no one, protests or applauds along with everyone else, and lives like a swallow, slipping in where he can.

He lives two steps away from his parish church, and in case of an important ceremony he can leave an assistant at his post and sing a requiem in the church choir. On Sundays and holidays he is its finest ornament, its most imposing voice, energetically opening his large mouth and thundering a joyous *Amen*. He is a choirmaster. Free at four o'clock from his official duties, he makes his appearance to spread joy and cheer in the most famous shop in the city. His wife is happy—he has no time to be jealous; he is a man of action, not feeling. And from the moment he arrives, he teases the young ladies behind the counter whose sparkling eyes attract customers in droves. He enjoys himself among the fichus and finery, the muslin fashioned by these clever working girls. Or more often, before going home to dinner, he does something practical, copying a page from the register or delivering some overdue bill to the bailiff.

Every other day at six o'clock, he is faithfully at his post at the Opéra. The permanent basso in the chorus, he is ready to transform himself into a soldier, an Arab, a prisoner, a native, a peasant, a ghost, one leg of a camel, a lion, a devil, a genie, a slave, a eunuch, black or white, always expert at imitating joy, sorrow, pity, surprise, shouting or falling silent on cue, hunting, fighting, representing Rome or Egypt; but at heart he is still a haberdasher. At midnight he again becomes a good husband, a man, a loving father. He slips into the conjugal bed, his imagination still captured by ephemeral visions of nymphs at the Opéra, and he turns the world's depravities and la Taglioni's voluptuous legs to the profit of conjugal love. Finally, if he does sleep, he sleeps in a rush, hurrying through his sleep as he hurries through his life.

All this activity makes man, who is space incarnate, the Proteus of civilization. This man embodies everything: history, literature, politics, government, religion, military art. He is a living encyclopedia, a grotesque atlas, forever on the march, never at rest, like Paris itself. He is all legs. No physiognomy engaged in such efforts could preserve its purity. Perhaps the worker who dies of old age at thirty, his stomach embalmed by ever greater doses of brandy, will be found by some well-heeled philosophers to be happier than the haberdasher. One is knocked out by a single blow and the other declines by degrees. From his eight occupations, from his shoulders, his voice, his hands, his wife, and his business, this man draws—as from so much property—a number of children, an income of several thousand francs, and the most laborious happiness that ever delighted the heart of man. This modest fortune and these children, or rather the children, who mean everything to him, fall prey to the class immediately above him, to whom he commends his gold and his daughter, or his son, raised with some education and more cultivated than his father, who trains his sights on higher things. Often the younger son of a small shopkeeper aspires to enter the civil service.

This ambition leads us to the second Parisian sphere. Climb up a floor, then, and go to the mezzanine; or come down from the attic and linger on the fourth floor; in any case, enter the world of those who possess something. The results are the same: Wholesalers and their boys, civil servants, small bankers of great honesty, rogues and rascals, head clerks and errand boys, the bailiff's bookkeeper, the lawyer, the notary, indeed the seething, scheming, speculating members of that lower middle class that caters to the demands of Paris and stays on the alert, hoarding provisions, handling products manufactured by the proletariat, dealing in fruit from the Midi, fish from the sea, wines from every sun-kissed slope. This class reaches out its hands to the Orient, takes shawls the Turks and Russians discard, casts its net as far as the Indies, waits for sales and looks for bargains, discounts bills of exchange and rolls along, gathering everything of value. It wraps up all of Paris bit by bit and carts it off, on the alert for the fantasies of childhood, spying out the whims and vices of maturity, and extorting advantage from its disease. Well, though they do not drink brandy like the worker or wallow in the mire on the outskirts of town, they too sap their strength, abuse their bodies and spirits, burn themselves up with desire, and destroy themselves, rushing headlong through life. In this case their bodies are twisted by the lash of self-interest and the scourge of ambition that torments the upper worlds of this monstrous city, just as the proletariat is crushed under the cruel wheel of proliferating production demanded by the despotic aristocracy and its incessant *I want*.

In this sphere, too, in order to obey that universal master, pleasure or gold, a man must devour time, hurry time, find more than twenty-four hours in the day, exhaust himself, work himself to death to sell thirty years of old age for two years of ailing repose. But the worker dies in the hospice when the last round of his stunted life has played itself out, while the petty bourgeois persists in living, and does live, cretinized. You meet him with his worn face, flattened, aged, dull-eyed, his legs frail, dragging himself in a daze along the boulevard, the girdle of his Venus, of his dear city. What did this bourgeois gentleman want? The National Guard saber, a full stockpot, a decent plot in Père-Lachaise Cemetery, and for his old age a little honestly won gold. The workman's Monday is Sunday for him. His relaxation is a drive in a hired carriage, a country outing so that his wife and children might happily swallow dust or roast in the sun. His destination is the restaurant famous for its poisonous food or a family ball where they swelter till midnight.

Certain simpletons are surprised by the St. Vitus' dance performed by the organisms visible in a drop of water under a microscope, but what would Rabelais's Gargantua say—that sublime, audacious, misunderstood figure—if he were to fall from the celestial spheres and amuse himself by contemplating the activities of this second level of Parisian life we have just described? Have you ever seen those little booths, cold in summer and heated in winter by only a small stove, under the vast copper dome that covers the Corn Exchange? Madame is there from early morning. She is an auctioneer at Les Halles, the farmer's market, and earns, they say, twelve thousand francs a year. When Madame rises, Monsieur moves into a gloomy office where he makes short-term loans to the neighborhood shopkeepers. At nine o'clock he is at the passport office, where he is one of the assistant directors. In the evening he is at the box office at the Théâtre-Italien, or at any other theater you care to choose. The children are put out to nurse, and return home only to attend lycée or boarding school. Monsieur and Madame live on a third floor, have only a cook, and give balls in a twelve-by eight-foot salon lit by oil lamps. But they give a dowry of a hundred and fifty thousand francs to their daughter and relax at the age of fifty, when they begin to appear in the third-tier boxes at the Opéra, in a hackney cab at the Longchamp races, or on sunny days in rather faded clothes on the boulevards: The espalier has borne fruit. Monsieur is admired in his quarter, esteemed by the government, allied to the upper middle class; at the age of sixty-five he obtains the cross of the Legion of Honor, and his son-in-law's father, the mayor of a district, invites him to his receptions. These efforts of a lifetime pay off for the children, whom this petty bourgeois invariably tends to raise to the next social level. Each sphere thus casts all its spawn into the sphere immediately above it. The rich grocer's son becomes a notary, the timber merchant's son a magistrate. Every cog falls into its groove, and everything stimulates the upward progress of money.

This brings us to the third circle of this inferno, which may one day find its Dante. In this third social circle, a kind of Parisian belly in which the interests of the city are digested and condensed into a form known as *affairs*, the crowd of lawyers, doctors, notaries, barristers, business men, bankers, manufacturers, speculators, and magistrates are stirred and shaken by an acidic and bitter intestinal movement. Here we encounter still more causes for physical and moral destruction than elsewhere. Almost all these men live in foul offices, contaminated court rooms, small cubicles with barred windows, and spend their days bent under the weight of their affairs, rising at dawn so as not to be cheated, to win all or not to lose, to seize a man or his money, to initiate or abort a business deal, grasp a fleeting opportunity, get a man hanged or acquitted. They take this out on their horses, they ruin them, overtax them, wear their legs out before their time—and their own as well. Time is their tyrant; they never have enough of it and it slips through their fingers; they cannot stretch it or shrink it.

What soul could remain great, pure, moral and

generous, what face could retain its beauty in the degrading exercise of a profession that makes it obligatory to bear the burden of public miseries, to analyze them, weigh them, appraise them, and process them systematically? Where do these men leave their hearts? I do not know; but when they have one, they set it aside before descending every morning to the pit of pain into which families are constantly pulled. There are no mysteries for them, they see the underside of the society whose confessors they are, and they despise it. Now, whatever they do, by dealing with corruption they are horrified by it and it saddens them, or out of weariness, out of some secret compromise, they accept it. In the end, of necessity they become cynical about all feeling, forced as they are by laws, men, and institutions to hover like vultures over still-warm corpses.

At all hours the man of money weighs the living, the man of contracts weighs the dead, the man of law weighs the conscience. Compelled to speak unceasingly, they all replace ideas with words, feelings with phrases, and their soul becomes their larynx. They are worn out and demoralized. Neither the wealthy merchant nor the judge nor the lawyer preserves his sense of integrity: They have no more feeling, they merely apply the rules that cash abrogates. Carried away by their torrential existence, they are neither husbands, fathers, nor lovers. They glide as in a sleigh over the things of life, and live every hour driven by the affairs of the great city. When they come home, they must go out to the ball, to the Opéra, to gatherings where they meet new clients, contacts, protectors. They all overeat, gamble, keep late hours, and their faces grow coarse, ruddy, and dull. For this terrible waste of intellectual energy, these manifold moral contradictions, they shore themselves up not with pleasure, which is too pale a contrast, but with debauchery, a secret and terrifying debauchery, for they have every means at their disposal and write society's moral code. Their real stupidity is hidden behind a specialized knowledge. They know their profession, but they are ignorant of everything outside it.

So to salvage their self-respect they question everything and criticize without rhyme or reason; they pose as skeptics and are in reality simpletons, drowning their wits in endless arguments. Nearly all of them readily adopt social, literary, or political prejudices in order to dispense with having an opinion, just as their consciences take refuge in the Civil Code or the commercial court. After starting out early to be remarkable men, they become mediocrities and scale the heights of society. And their faces present that acute pallor, that unnatural coloring, those dull, hollow eyes, those gossiping, sensual mouths in which the observer recognizes the symptoms of degenerate thinking, spinning within the boundaries of a specialization that kills the generative faculties of the brain, the gift of seeing the larger picture, of generalizing and deducing. Almost all these men are shriveled in the furnace of affairs. And a man who lets himself be caught in the gears of these immense machines can never become great. If he is a doctor, either he practices very little medicine or he is an exception, a Bichat who dies young. If he is a great merchant and retains his importance, he is almost a Jacques Coeur. Did Robespierre ever practice law? Was Danton simply lazy, waiting around for something to happen? But who has ever envied figures such as Danton and Robespierre, superb as they may have been?

These preeminent men of affairs attract money and amass it to form alliances with aristocratic families. If the working man and the clerk have identical ambitions, here again the same passions reign. In Paris, vanity is the sum of all passions. The typical man of this class would be either the ambitious burgher, who after a life of stressful effort and continuous maneuvering manages to enter the Council of State the way an ant enters through a crack in the wall; some newspaper editor, an old hand at intrigues, whom the King makes a peer of France, perhaps to take revenge on the nobility; or a notary who becomes mayor of his district. All these men are warped and hardened by affairs, and if they reach their goal, they are half dead by the time they do. The practice in France is to enthrone the old fogies. Napoleon, Louis XIV, the great kings always wanted young men to carry out their plans.

Above this sphere is the world of the artist. But here, too, faces marked by the stamp of originality are nobly shattered, but shattered nonetheless, exhausted and tortured. Overworked by a need to produce, burdened by their costly fantasies, weakened by a consuming genius, avid for pleasure, the artists of Paris all make overweening efforts to fill the gaps left by their idleness, and try in vain to reconcile society and fame, money and art. In the beginning the artist is always harassed by creditors; his needs generate his debts, and his debts take up his nights. After work comes pleasure. The actor performs until midnight, studies his part in the morning, rehearses at midday. The sculptor bends over his statue; the journalist is thought on the march, like a soldier going to war; the fashionable painter is overwhelmed with work, while the painter without commissions eats his heart out if he thinks he is a man of genius. Competition, rivalries, slander destroy these talents. Some of these men, in despair, slide into the pit of vice, others die young and unknown because they had counted on success too soon. Few of these faces, originally sublime, retain their beauty. In any case their dazzling beauty goes unacknowledged. An artist's face is always extraordinary; it is always above or below the conventional lines of what fools call ideal beauty. What force destroys them? Passion. In Paris every passion is resolved into two terms: gold or pleasure.

Now, can you breathe? Can you feel the purer air and space? Up here there are no projects or pains. The spinning spiral of gold has reached the heights. From under the airshafts where its channels begin, from the meager coffers of shops where it is temporarily halted, from within the counting houses and great foundries where it is melted into bars, gold, in the form of dowries or legacies, carried by the hands of young girls or by the bony hands of old men, gushes toward the tribe of the aristocracy where it glitters, spreads, and streams. But before leaving the four social realms on which the great wealth of Paris depends, we should, after enumerating moral causes, deduce physical causes and call attention to an underlying plague that perpetually afflicts the faces of the porter, the shopkeeper, and the artisan; we should point out the deleterious influence whose corruption is equal to that of the Parisian administrators who complacently allow it to persist. If the air of the houses where most of the middle class live is foul, if the atmosphere of the streets spews terrible vapors into airless backrooms, you must realize that in addition to this pestilence forty thousand buildings of this great city stand in filth which the authorities have not yet seriously thought to confine in concrete walls that might prevent the most fetid muck from filtering through the soil, poisoning wells and making its name, Lutetia*, still famous, at least underground. Half of Paris lives in the putrid fumes of courtyards, streets, and sewers.

But let us enter the great airy, gilded salons, the mansions set in gardens, the world of wealth—idle, happy, and financially independent. The faces here are sickly, consumed by vanity. Here, nothing is real. Doesn't the search for pleasure always end in boredom? The fashionable folk have twisted their natures at an early age. Occupied with nothing but the pursuit of pleasure, they have been quick to abuse their senses, as the worker abuses his brandy. Pleasure is like certain medicinal substances: To maintain the same effects you must double the dose, and this in-

---

*In Celtic, "a place in the swamps."

evitably leads to death or brutishness. All the lower classes cower before the rich and are alert to their tastes in order to turn them into vices and exploit them. How can one resist the skillful seductions practiced in this land? Paris, too, has its opium-eaters, and their opium is gambling, gastrolatry, or fornication. And you see these people at an early age develop taste, not passions, romantic fantasies and cold-blooded love affairs. Here, impotence reigns; here, ideas no longer exist: They are dissipated like energy in the affectations of the boudoir, in feminine antics. There are callow youths of forty and pompous old men of sixteen. In Paris the rich embrace ready-made wit, predigested knowledge, preformed opinions that exempt them from the need for wit, knowledge, or opinion. In this world, foolishness is as conspicuous as weakness and licentiousness. They waste time with such abandon, they have none to spare. Don't look for affections here, any more than for ideas. Embraces conceal a profound indifference, and politeness an unrelieved contempt. No one here is capable of loving his fellow man. Shallow witticisms, indiscretions, malicious gossip, and especially platitudes—this is their talk. But these unfortunate *fortunates* disclaim that they come together merely to invent and intone maxims in the manner of La Rochefoucauld, as if there were no middle ground, established in the eighteenth century, between hyperbole and utter vacuousness. If a few able men indulge in refined and subtle humor, it is not understood; and soon, weary of giving without receiving, they stay home, leaving the dunces to lord it over their turf. This empty life, this constant anticipation of unfulfilled pleasure, this permanent boredom, this frivolity of mind, heart, and brain, this weariness with the great Parisian receptions is mirrored in their features and produces those cardboard faces, those premature wrinkles, that physiognomy of the rich in which impotence grins, gold is reflected, and intelligence has fled.

This view of moral Paris proves that physical Paris could not be other than it is. This city with its diadem is a perpetually pregnant queen who has irresistibly imperative desires. Paris is the mind of the globe, a brain full of genius at the head of civilization, a great man, an ever creative artist, a politician with second sight, and must of necessity have the wrinkles of a great mind, the vices of a great man, the fantasies of an artist, and the cynicism of a politician. Its physiognomy implies the flowering of good and evil, conflict and victory: the moral battle of 1789, whose trumpets still resound in every corner of the world, and also the defeat of 1814.

This city, then, can have no greater morality, friendly feeling, or cleanliness than the boiler engines of those magnificent steamships that you admire as they cut through the waves! Paris is indeed a superb vessel laden with intelligence. Yes, her coat of arms is one of those oracles sometimes allowed by fate. The CITY OF PARIS has her tall bronze mast engraved with victories and with Napoleon at the helm. This craft may pitch and roll, but she plows through the world of men, fires through the hundred mouths of her tribunes, furrows the seas of science full steam ahead, cries from the height of her topsails through the voices of her scholars and artists: "Forward, march! Follow me!"

She carries a vast crew that enjoys decking her out in new streamers. There are cabin boys and errand boys laughing in the rigging; her ballast is the sturdy middle class; there are workers and old tars; and in their cabins, the happy passengers. Elegant midshipmen smoke their cigars, leaning over the railing; then on the main deck, her soldiers, innovators, or men of ambition, are ready to land on every shore and, while spreading their bright rays, demand the pleasure of glory or love bought with gold.

So it is that the excessive activities of the working class, the depraved interests that crush the two middle classes, the torments of artistic thought, and the surfeit of pleasure incessantly sought by the great explain the customary ugliness of the Parisian physiognomy. Only in the Orient does the human race present a magnificent aspect; but this is a result of the constant calm cultivated by those profound philosophers with their long pipes, short legs, and barrel chests, who disdain activity of any kind. Whereas in Paris, small, medium, and large run, jump, and caper about, lashed by a merciless goddess, Need: the need for money, glory, or amusement. Any fresh, rested, graceful, truly young face is the most extraordinary of exceptions, and rarely encountered. If you see one, it most certainly belongs to a young, idealistic cleric or to some good, middle-aged parish priest with a triple chin; to an innocent young lady of the sort raised in certain bourgeois families; to a twenty-year-old mother, still full of illusions, nursing her firstborn; to a young man newly arrived from the provinces and entrusted to the care of a pious old lady who keeps him short of money; or perhaps to some shop boy, who goes to sleep at midnight, exhausted from folding or unfolding calico, and rises at seven in the morning to arrange the window display. Often it belongs to a man of science or poetry, who lives a monastic existence enriched by a noble idea, who lives soberly, patiently, and chastely; or even to some self-satisfied blockhead feeding on his own stupidity, bursting with health, always busy smiling to himself; or to that happy, languid species of loafers, the only truly happy men in Paris, who savor every hour of its hectic poetry.

Nonetheless, there is in Paris a group of privileged beings who profit from this excessive activity of manufacturing, interests, business affairs, arts, and gold. These are the women. Although they too have a thousand secret causes that here, more than elsewhere, destroy their physiognomy, in the feminine world one meets small, happy bands of women who live in the Oriental fashion and are able to preserve their beauty. But these women rarely show themselves on foot in the streets; they remain hidden, like rare plants that unfold their petals only at certain hours, and constitute exotic exceptions.

Yet Paris is essentially a land of contrasts. If true feelings are rare, noble friendships do exist, and even boundless devotions. On this battlefield of interests and passions, as in those societies on the march where egotism triumphs and it's every man for himself—we call these *armies*—it seems that feelings, when they are shown, are given full expression and are, by contrast, sublime. So it is with faces. In Paris, in the upper levels of the aristocracy, one sometimes sees scattered here and there a few ravishing young men, the fruit of quite an exceptional breeding and upbringing. They unite the youthful beauty of English blood with the strength of southern features, French wit, and purity of form. The fire in their eyes, a delicious blush on their lips, the shimmering black of their silken hair, a fair complexion, a distinguished profile make them lovely human flowers, magnificent to see against the mass of leaden, withered, warped, and cringing physiognomies. And women instantly admire these young men with that avid pleasure men take in looking at a pretty girl who is virtuous and graceful, endowed with all the virginal charms our imagination loves to ascribe to the perfect young lady.

If this quick glance at the population of Paris has helped you to understand the rarity of a Raphaelesque face and the passionate admiration it must inspire at first sight, the main purpose of our story has been achieved. *Quod erat demonstrandum*: This had to be demonstrated, if I may be allowed to apply the formulas of scholasticism to the science of manners.

*N*ow, on one of those beautiful spring mornings when the leaves are not yet green though beginning to unfurl, when the sun is just setting the rooftops afire and the sky is blue, when the Parisian population is leaving its hives and comes buzzing down the boulevards or glides like a multicolored snake along the Rue de la Paix toward the Tuileries in honor of the courtship rituals begun once again in the countryside—on one of these joyful days a graceful young man, handsome as the day is long and tastefully dressed, a love child (we shall tell his secret), the natural son of Lord Dudley and the famous Marquise de Vordac, was strolling along the main avenue of the Tuileries. This Adonis, whose name was Henri de Marsay, was born in France where Lord Dudley had come to marry off the young woman, already Henri's mother, to an old gentleman called Monsieur de Marsay. This faint and fading butterfly recognized the child as his own in return for the interest on an income of a hundred

27

thousand francs to be settled on his putative son, an extravagance that Lord Dudley could easily afford since French stocks were then worth seventeen francs fifty. The old gentleman died without having known his wife. Madame de Marsay then married the Marquis de Vordac; but even before becoming Marquise she had shown little concern for either her child or Lord Dudley. First of all, the war declared between France and England had separated the two lovers, and fidelity was not and hardly ever will be the fashion in Paris. Then, the success of the elegant, pretty, universally adored woman dampened the Parisian's maternal feeling. Lord Dudley was no more solicitous of his progeny than was the boy's mother. Perhaps the prompt infidelity of a girl so passionately loved gave him a kind of aversion to everything belonging to her. And it may be that fathers only love the children they know well: This is a social belief of crucial importance to a family's peace of mind, one all bachelors must support by proving that paternity is a feeling cultivated in a hothouse by women, customs, and laws.

Poor Henri de Marsay knew only the father who was not obliged to be one. Monsieur de Marsay's paternity was, of course, very incomplete. In the natural order of things, children have a father for only a few moments; and that gentleman imitated nature.

The good man would not have sold his name if he'd had no vices. So he ate with impunity in gambling dens and drank up elsewhere the half-yearly dividend which the National Treasury paid to its bondholders. Then he handed the child over to an aged sister, who on the meager pension her brother gave her provided the boy with a tutor—a penniless priest who calculated the young man's future and resolved to pay himself out of an expected income of a hundred thousand pounds for the care he lavished, with genuine affection, on his charming pupil.

This tutor just happened to be a real priest, one of those ecclesiastics with the makings of a French cardinal or a Borgia candidate for the papacy. He taught the boy in three years what it would have taken ten to learn at school. Then this great man, the Abbé de Maronis, completed his pupil's education by making him study civilization in all its aspects. He gave him the benefit of his own experience, which involved very few church visits (the churches were closed at the time). He sometimes took him to the theater, often backstage, and still more frequently to the houses of courtesans. He paraded before him the array of human emotions, taught him politics in salons sizzling with intrigue, explained the machinery of government, and tried, out of friendship for a fine nature, forsaken but rich in hope, to be a virile mother-substitute—for after all, isn't the Church the mother of orphans?

The pupil responded to such solicitous care. This worthy man died a bishop in 1812, satisfied at leaving behind a child whose heart and mind were so well-formed by the age of sixteen that he could outsmart a man of forty. Who would have expected to meet a heart of bronze and a brain like a steel trap in a boy endowed with features as seductive as those the naive old painters attributed to the serpent in the earthly paradise? And that's not all. In addition, the old devil in bishop's garb had introduced his favorite child to certain acquaintances in Parisian high society who were worth another hundred thousand pounds in the young man's hands. Indeed, this corrupt but politic priest, unbelieving but wise, treacherous but aimiable, apparently weak but as strong in mind as in body, was so practically useful to his student, so indulgent of his vices, such a good judge of strength, so shrewd at allowing for human weakness, so hearty at table, that by 1814 almost the only thing that could move the grateful Henri de Marsay was his dear bishop's portrait. This was the prelate's sole tangible legacy, admirable man that he was, the type whose genius will save the Roman apostolic church, now compromised by the feebleness of its recruits and the dotage of its pontiffs. But that is the Church's choice.

The Continental war prevented the young de Marsay from knowing his real father; it is doubtful he even knew his name. As an abandoned child, he was equally unacquainted with Madame de Marsay. Naturally, he felt little regret for his adoptive father. As for Madame de Marsay, the only mother he had known, he erected a pretty little monument for her at Père-Lachaise Cemetery when she died. Monsignor de Maronis had guaranteed the old spinster one of the best places in heaven, so that seeing how happy she was to die, Henri shed selfish tears, weeping chiefly for his own sake. Seeing this sorrow, the Abbé dried his pupil's tears by reminding him that the old girl had been taking her tobacco quite disgustingly, and had grown so ugly, so deaf, so tedious of late that he owed death a debt of thanks.

By 1811 the bishop had released his student. Then, when Monsieur de Marsay's mother remarried, the priest called a family council and entrusted one of those honest idiots, whom he had further tested in the confessional, to administer the young man's fortune, applying the income to general necessities while keeping the capital intact.

Toward the end of 1814, then, Henri de Marsay

felt no earthly obligation and was free as a bird. Although he had reached the age of twenty-two, he looked scarcely seventeen. Generally, even his most prickly rivals conceded that he was the handsomest young man in Paris. From his father, Lord Dudley, he had inherited the most amorously enchanting blue eyes; from his mother, thick curly black hair; from both parents pure blood, a girlish complexion, a gentle and modest manner, a slim and aristocratic figure, and beautiful hands. A woman would take one look at him and fall head over heels—you know?—her heart consumed by one of those desires that is nonetheless forgotten because it is impossible to satisfy, since Paris women are not commonly tenacious. Few say to themselves, as men do, "*I will uphold* the house of Orange." Beneath this youthful freshness and the limpid clarity of his eyes, Henri had a lion's courage, a monkey's agility. He could cut a bullet in half at ten paces on the blade of a knife, sit a horse like the fabled centaur, and gracefully handle the lead reins of a carriage; he was as nimble as Cherubin and as cool as a cucumber; but he knew how to beat a street fighter at the terrible games of foot-boxing or quarterstaffs. Furthermore, he played the piano so well he could have become a performer had he fallen onto hard times, and possessed a voice for which any impressario would have paid fifty thousand francs a season. Alas, all these fine qualities and charming defects were tarnished by one dreadful vice: He believed in neither men nor women, God nor the Devil. Capricious Nature had given him gifts; a priest had finished the task.

To make this adventure comprehensible, we must add here that Lord Dudley naturally found many women disposed to make a few copies of such a charming portrait. His second masterpiece of this kind was a young girl called Euphémie, the daughter of a Spanish lady, raised in Havana, taken to Madrid with a young Creole from the Antilles, both of them with the colonies' ruinous tastes. Happily, however, she was married to an old and immensely rich Spanish lord, Don Hijos, Marquis de San-Réal, who since the occupation of Spain by French troops had come to live in Paris, on Rue Saint-Lazare. As much out of heedlessness as out of respect for the innocence of their youth, Lord Dudley gave his children no information about the relationships he was creating for them everywhere. This is one of those small inconveniences of civilization which has such advantages that its benefits must surely outweigh its deficits. Now Lord Dudley, and this is the last we'll hear of him, came to Paris in 1816 to take refuge from English justice, which protects nothing from the Orient but merchandise. Seeing Henri, the peripatetic lord asked who this handsome young man was. Then, hearing his name, he declared: "Ah! he's my son. What a shame!"

Such was the history of the young man who, around the middle of April, 1815, was strolling nonchalantly down the main avenue of the Tuileries with the majestic calm of an animal confident in its strength. Bourgeois women naively turned to catch another glimpse of him; society women did not turn around but waited for his return, engraving those features upon their memories so as to remember the charming face that would not have disgraced even the most beautiful among them.

"What are you doing here on a Sunday?" the Marquis de Ronquerolles remarked to Henri as he passed.

"There are fish in the pond," the young man answered.

This exchange of thoughts was made by means of knowing looks, with neither Ronquerolles nor de Marsay appearing to recognize each other. The young man examined the passersby with that ready glance and fine-tuned ear peculiar to the Parisian who seems neither to see nor hear but who sees and hears everything. At this moment, another young man came up to him and took him familiarly by the arm, saying: "How's it going, my good de Marsay?"

"Oh, pretty well," de Marsay replied with that air of apparent affection which between young Parisians means nothing, either in the present or the future.

Indeed, the young men of Paris are unlike the young men of any other city. They are divided into two categories: the young man who has something, and the young man who has nothing; or the young man who ponders and the one who squanders. But you must understand, this applies only to those natives of Paris who set the delicious pace of an elegant life. There are certainly other sorts of young men here, but these fellows are like children who come to understand Parisian life very late and remain its dupes. They do not speculate—they study, they are grinds, as the others say. Indeed, if there are still certain young people, whether rich or poor, who embrace careers and doggedly pursue them, they are a little like Rousseau's Emile, ordinary citizens, and never appear in good society. The diplomatic rudely call them ninnies. Ninnies or not, they swell the ranks of the mediocrities who weigh France down. They are always there with the flat trowel of their mediocrity, always ready to bungle public or private concerns, taking pride in their impotence, which they call convention and honesty. These social prizewinners infest the civil service, the army, the magistrature, the law offices, the court. They soften and flatten the country, and constitute, as it were, a lymph in the body politic, overloading it and bloating it. These honest citizens call men of talent libertines or rogues. These rogues make their services pay but at least they serve, while the others do harm. They are respected by the crowd, but happily for France the gilded youth always stigmatize them as fools.

At first glance, then, it is natural to believe in the clear distinction between the two sorts of young men who lead that elegant life so agreeably embodied by Henri de Marsay. But observers who look beneath the surface are soon convinced that the differences are purely moral, and that nothing is so deceptive as a pleasing exterior. Still, they all claim their superiority over the rest of the world; they talk at random of things, of men, of literature, of the fine arts, always mentioning each year's list of royalist enemies. They will interrupt a conversation with a pun, ridicule science and the scientist, scorn everything they don't know or everything they fear, and set themselves up as judges in all matters, great and small. They are ready to dupe their fathers and to weep crocodile tears on their mothers' shoulders; but generally they believe in nothing, curse women or display false modesty, while in reality submitting to some cunning courtesan or old hag. They are all rotten to the core with calculation, depravity, a brutal passion to succeed in society, and if they suffered from stones, these would be found not in their kidneys but in their hearts.

In their normal state they are most pleasing on the outside, quite captivating, and willing to stake friendship at every turn. The same mean-spirited banter dominates their ever-changing slang. They vie for eccentricity in dress, glory in repeating the nonsense of the latest fashionable actor, and any one of them would be scornful or impertinent enough to make the first move in this game. But woe to him who does not know how to lose one round in order to win two! They seem equally indifferent to the misfortunes of their homeland and its enemies. Indeed, they are all like the lovely white foam that crests the stormy waves. They would dress, dine, dance, and amuse themselves on the day of Waterloo, during a cholera epidemic or a revolution.

To sum things up, they all have the same expenses, but here we see some difference. Some have the capital of this fluctuating fortune, so agreeably thrown away, while others are still expecting it; they use the same tailors, but their bills are outstanding. Then again, if some of them, like sieves, entertain all sorts of ideas without keeping any in their heads, the others compare them and assimilate the good ones. If some of them, thinking they know something, know nothing but pretend to understand everything, lend freely to those who need nothing but offer nothing to those in need, the others secretly study other people's thoughts and invest their money, as they do their follies, for the highest interest on their return. Some of them no longer register accurate impressions of things because their soul, like a mirror tarnished from use, no longer reflects an image; others spare their senses and their life while seeming, like their fellows, to squander them.

The first type, on the strength of his hopes, devotes himself halfheartedly to a system subject to wind and tide, but jumps onto another political craft when the first goes adrift. The second type calculates the future, analyzes it, and sees in political fidelity what the English see in commercial probity—an element of success. But where the young man who has something makes a pun or tells a joke on the veerings of the throne, the man who has nothing engages in a public calculation, or some secret intrigue, and comes out ahead by greasing the palms of his friends. The first sort never believes in the abilities of others and thinks his own ideas are original, as if the world were made yesterday; he has unlimited confidence in himself and is his own worst enemy. But the other, while he mistrusts men on principle, judges them at their true worth and is shrewd enough to stay one step ahead of his friends, whom he exploits. Then, in the evenings, when he lays his head on his pillow, he weighs men as a miser weighs pieces of gold. The first is vexed by a trivial slight but allows himself to be gulled by the diplomat, who makes him dance like a puppet by pulling the string of his vanity. Men like this know how to gain respect and how to choose their victims and their protectors. So one fine day, those who had nothing have something; and those who had something, have nothing. They regard their newly successful friends as cunning and corrupt, but also as men of ability. "He is a man of real ability!" This is the great testimony to those who have succeeded, *qui buscumque viis*, in politics, in love, or in fortune. Among them there are certain young men who are in debt when they take up this role, and of course they are more dangerous than those who play it penniless.

The young man who called himself the friend of Henri de Marsay was a callow youth from the provinces who was learning from the fashionable young men of the time the art of running through an inheritance. But he had a last resource to fall back on: a settled estate in his native province. He was simply an heir who had gone without transition from his meager hundred francs a month to the entire paternal fortune, and who, though he may not have had the sense to see that he was laughed at, knew enough to stop at two-thirds of his capital. For the price of a few thousand francs he had discovered in Paris the exact cost of harnesses, the art of being less respectful of his gloves, shrewd advice on the proper wages for servants and tradesmen, and how to find the best bargain for their services. He set great store in speaking highly of his horses and his Pyrenees dog; recognizing a woman's station by her dress, her walk, and her shoes; learning how to play Écarté; picking up a few fashionable witticisms; and gaining by his sojourn in Parisian society the necessary authority to import to the provinces a taste for tea and English silver, and the right to despise everything around him for the rest of his days. De Marsay had befriended him in order to make use of him in society, the way a bold speculator makes use of a private accountant. De Marsay's friendship, real or not, provided a social position for Paul de Manerville, who firmly believed, on his part, that he was exploiting his close friend in his own way. He lived in his friend's reflection, constantly took refuge beneath his umbrella, followed in his footsteps, and basked in his glory. Standing near him or even walking beside him, he seemed to say: "Don't insult us, we're real tigers." He was often fatuous enough to say: "Henri is such a close friend of mine, he would do me any favor I ask . . ." But he was careful never to ask him for anything. He was afraid of him, and his fear, though barely perceptible, affected others and was useful to de Marsay. "He's one in a million, de Marsay," Paul would say. "Ah, you'll see, he'll be whatever he wants. I wouldn't be surprised to see him become foreign minister one of these days. Nothing can stop him." Then he made of de Marsay what Corporal Trim made of his cap: the stakes of every wager. "Ask de Marsay, and you'll see!"

Or else: "The other day we were out hunting, de Marsay and I. He wouldn't believe I could do it, but I jumped a hedge without falling off my horse!"

Or: "We were keeping company with some women, de Marsay and I, and upon my word of honor, I was . . ." and so on.

Thus Paul de Manerville could be classified among that great, illustrious, and powerful family of ninnies who manage to succeed. One day he would be a deputy. For the moment, he was not even a young man. His friend defined him this way: "You ask me what Paul is? Paul? Why, he is Paul de Manerville."

"My dear fellow," said he to de Marsay, "I'm surprised to see you here on a Sunday."

"I was going to say the same to you."

"An affair?"

"Perhaps . . ."

"Come now!"

"I can mention this to you without compromising my passion. Anyway, a woman who comes to the Tuileries on Sundays has no cachet, from an aristocratic viewpoint."

"Ha, ha!"

"Keep quiet or I'll tell you nothing. You laugh too loudly, you'll make people think we've drunk too much at lunch. Last Thursday, I was strolling here on the terrace of Feuillant's, thinking of nothing in particular. But when I reached the gate at Rue Castiglione, intending to leave, I found myself face to face with a woman, or rather with a young girl who, if she didn't throw her arms around my neck at any rate stopped short, gripped less, I believe, by a sense of decorum than by one of those moments of profound surprise that paralyze the limbs, travel the length of the spine, and nail your feet to the ground. I've often produced effects of this kind, a sort of animal magnetism that becomes enormously powerful when affinities are strong. But my dear fellow, this was not a case of stupefaction nor was she a common girl. Morally speaking, her face seemed to say: 'What—there you are, my ideal, the creature I've thought of, dreamed of morning and night. How can you be here? Why this morning? Why not yesterday?

Take me, I'm yours!' etc. 'Good,' I said to myself, 'another one!' Then I took a close look at her. Ah, my dear boy, physically speaking, this stranger is the most adorable woman I've ever met. She belongs to that variety of the feminine the Romans called *fulva flava*—the woman of fire. And what struck me most, what still charms me, are her two yellow eyes like the eyes of a tiger; a gleaming yellow gold, a living gold, a thinking gold that loves and absolutely wants to get into your pocket!"

"My dear fellow, we're all mad about her!" cried Paul. "She comes here sometimes. She's the *girl with the golden eyes*—that's our name for her. She's a young woman of around twenty-two, and I saw her here under the Bourbons, but with a woman a hundred thousand times better."

"Quiet, Paul! No woman could possibly surpass this girl. She's like a kitten that rubs itself against your legs, a light-skinned girl with dark hair, delicate-looking but surely with feathery tufts on the ends of her fingers. And along her cheeks a white down that shimmers in the light, starting at her ears and running down her neck."

"Ah, but the other one, my dear de Marsay, has ruthless, burning black eyes, black eyebrows joined in the middle that give her a hardness belied by the pouting line of her lips, lips made for kisses, cool and passionate, and a Moorish complexion that warms a man like the sun. But upon my word of honor, she looks like you . . ."

"You flatter her!"

"Her figure is firm, sleek as a little navy craft, the kind built for speed that runs down a merchant ship with French impetuosity, catches it, and sinks it in no time."

"Well, my dear fellow," answered de Marsay, "I'm not interested in a woman I've never seen. I've studied women for some time, and my unknown girl is the only one whose virgin breast and ardent, sensuous shape embody the woman of my dreams! She is the original of that ravishing painting, 'Woman Caressing Her Dream,' the most impassioned, infernal inspiration of antique genius—a sacred poem debased by those who have copied it in frescoes and mosaics for bourgeois gentlemen who regard this exquisite cameo as nothing but a trinket and wear copies of it on their watch chains. She is really the essence of woman, an endless abyss of pleasure, an ideal woman who is sometimes really found in Spain or Italy, but almost never in France. Ah well, I saw that young girl with the golden eyes again, that woman caressing her dream, I saw her here on Friday. I was sure she would come again the next day at the same time. I was not mistaken. I amused myself by following her without being seen, studying her indolent walk, the walk of an idle woman who exudes a dormant sensuality. Well, she turned around, she saw me, looked adoringly at me once more, trembling and shivering. Then I noticed the genuine Spanish duenna accompanying her, a hyena, some jealous man dressed like a woman, some she-devil paid to guard this sweet creature . . . Oh, that duenna made me more than amorous, I grew curious. On Saturday, no one came. So here I am today, waiting for the girl whose dream I have become, asking nothing better than to pose as the monster in the fresco."

"There she is," said Paul. "Everyone is turning to look at her . . ."

The unknown girl blushed. Her eyes shone when she glimpsed Henri; she closed them and passed by.

"She notices you, does she?" cried Paul facetiously.

The duenna stared attentively at the two young men. When Henri and the unknown girl passed each other again, the young girl brushed against him and pressed the young man's hand in hers. Then she turned to him and smiled passionately, but the duenna quickly led her away toward the gate at Rue Castiglione. The two friends followed the girl, admiring the magnificent curve of her neck, which was joined to her head in a harmony of vigorous lines, softened by several thick curls of escaping hair. The girl with the golden eyes had that sort of shapely foot, narrow and curving, that is so attractive to the sensitive imagination. Moreover, she was elegantly shod and wore a short dress. During her passage she turned around every so often to give Henri a backward glance, and appeared reluctant to follow the old woman who seemed to be at once her mistress and her slave. It was clear that she might have thrashed the woman, but she could not send her away. The two friends reached the gate. Two livried footmen set down the step of a tasteful brougham emblazoned with armorial bearings. The girl with the golden eyes entered first and took a seat on the side where she could be seen when the carriage turned; she put her hand on the door and, unseen by the duenna, waved her handkerchief, indifferent to what the curious might say, as if telling Henri openly, "Follow me . . ."

"Have you ever seen a handkerchief waved so charmingly?" said Henri to Paul de Manerville.

Then, noticing a cab preparing to leave after dropping off a fare, he signaled the driver to wait.

"Follow that brougham," he said. "Find the street and the house it goes to and I'll give you ten francs. Good-bye, Paul."

The cab followed the brougham. The brougham returned to Rue Saint-Lazare and turned into one of the finest mansions in that quarter.

*D*e Marsay was not a fool. Any other young man would have surrendered to the desire to gather immediate information about a girl who so admirably embodied the most luminous notions of women expressed in Oriental poetry. But Henri was too clever to compromise his future happiness, and told his driver to continue along Rue Saint-Lazare to his own mansion. The next day his personal valet, Laurent, as sly a fellow as any servant in an eighteenth-century farce, waited near the house where the unknown girl was living, at the hour when the mail was usually delivered. So that he might spy and prowl around the house at will, he had followed the practice of police agents in disguise and, having purchased the cast-off clothing of someone from the Auvergne, did his best to impersonate their former owner. When the postman arrived that morning to deliver letters in Rue Saint-Lazare, Laurent consulted the fellow, pretending to be a commercial messenger with a parcel for a woman whose name he had momentarily forgotten. Initially fooled by appearances, the postman, a quaint fellow by Parisian standards, informed him that the mansion belonged to Don Hijos, the Marquis de San-Réal, grandee of Spain. Naturally the Auvergnat had no interest in the Marquis.

"My parcel," he said, "is for the Marquise."

"She is away," replied the postman. "Her letters are forwarded to London."

"So the Marquise is not a young girl who . . ."

"Ah!" said the postman, interrupting the valet and examining him closely, "If you're a messenger, I'm a dancer."

Laurent offered the civil servant several pieces of gold, and he began to smile.

"Look, here is the name of your quarry," he said, taking from his leather box a letter with a London stamp and this address:

to Mademoiselle
PAQUITA VALDES
Rue Saint-Lazare, Hotel de San-Réal
Paris

This was written in a spidery, elongated script that betrayed a feminine hand.

"Would you object to a bottle of Chablis, along with a steak sautéed in mushrooms, and starting with a dozen oysters?" said Laurent, who wanted to ensure the postman's friendship.

"At nine-thirty, after my work. Where?"

"At the corner of Rue de la Chaussée-d'Antin and Rue Neuve-des-Mathurins, '*Au Puits sans Vin*,'" said Laurent.

"Listen, friend," said the postman, joining the valet an hour after this meeting, "If your master is in love with this girl, he's looking for nothing but trouble! I doubt you'll even manage to see her. For the ten years I've been a postman in Paris, I've seen all the schemes people use to guard their doors! But I can say confidently, and none of my pals will call me a liar, that there isn't a door in the city as mysterious as Monsieur de San-Réal's. No one can enter the mansion without some password, and notice that he deliberately chose a house that sits between a courtyard and a garden to avoid any contact with other houses. The porter is an old Spaniard who never speaks a word of French; but he looks people over the way a police chief like Vidocq might do, to make sure they're not thieves.

"If a lover, a thief, or even you—no offense—could get by this watchdog in the first hall, which is closed by a glass door, you would encounter a majordomo surrounded by lackies, an old joker even more vicious and surly than the porter. If anyone gets through the main entrance, my majordomo comes out, waits for you on the porch, and interrogates you as if you were a criminal. It's happened to me, and I'm just a simple postman. He took me for a *messager* in disguise," he said, laughing at his own malapropism.

"As for the servants, don't waste your time trying to get anything out of them. I think they're mute. No one in the quarter has ever heard them speak, and I have no idea how much they must be paid never to talk and never to take a drink. The fact is, you can't approach them, either because they're afraid of being shot or because they stand to lose a pile if they slip up. If your master loves Mademoiselle Paquita Valdes enough to get past all these obstacles, he certainly won't get the better of Doña Concha Marialva, the duenna who chaperones her, and who would sooner put her under her skirts than let her out of her sight. Those two women look like they're sewn together."

"Everything you say, good postman," replied Laurent after tasting the wine, "confirm's what I've just heard. I honestly thought they were kidding me. The fruit seller across the way told me that at night they let dogs into the gardens and hang their food on stakes, just out of reach. Those miserable animals think that people trying to get into the garden are after their food and tear them to pieces. You might tell me I can throw them meatballs, but it seems they're trained to eat only from the hand of the porter."

"The porter at Monsieur le Baron de Nucingen's, whose upper garden borders on the San-Réal property, told me as much," replied the postman.

Good, Laurent said to himself, my master knows the Baron.

"You should know," he went on, gazing at the postman, "that my master is a determined man, and if he took it into his head to kiss the soles of an empress's feet, she would have to let him. If he needed your help, and I hope for your sake that he does, for he is very generous, could he count on you?"

"You bet! Monsieur Laurent, my name is Sparo. My name is written just like the bird: S-p-a-r-o, Sparo."

"Fine."

"I live at Eleven Rue des Trois-Frères, on the fifth floor. I've got a wife and four children. If what you want me to do isn't at odds with my conscience and my job, you understand—then I'm yours."

"Good man," said Laurent, shaking his hand.

"Paquita Valdes is probably the mistress of the Marquis de San-Réal, the friend of King Ferdinand. Only an old Spanish bag of bones would be capable of taking such precautions," Henri said when his valet told him the result of his inquiries.

"Monsieur," Laurent replied, "no one could get into that house unless he came in a balloon."

"You're a fool! Do I have to get into the house to have Paquita when she can come out?"

"But Monsieur, what about the duenna?"

"We'll lock her up for a few days."

"Then we shall have Paquita!" said Laurent, rubbing his hands together.

"Rascal!" Henri replied, "I'll throw you to la Concha if you're insolent enough to talk that way about a woman before I've had her. Now get busy dressing me, I'm going out."

Henri was plunged for a moment in joyous thoughts. To the credit of the female sex, it must be said that he possessed as many women as he desired. After all, what would we think of a woman without a lover who could resist a young man armed with beauty that is the intelligence of the body, with intelligence that is the grace of the soul, with moral strength and wealth that are the only two authentic powers? But de Marsay was sure to grow bored with such easy conquests; and indeed, for the past two years he had been feeling quite bored. Diving into the depths of sensual pleasures, he brought up more gravel than pearls. Like a lord of the realm, he implored chance to put some obstacle in his way that he might overcome, some undertaking that required the deployment of his dormant moral and physical strengths. Although Paquita Valdes offered a marvelous array of perfections, which he had as yet savored only one by one, passionate attachments held little attraction for him. A state of constant satiety had weakened the love in his heart. Like old men and surfeited roués, he now had only extravagant whims, ruinous tastes, and fantasies that, once satisfied, left no pleasant memories in his heart.

In young people, love is the finest of sentiments; it coaxes the soul to bloom and, like sunshine, its power enhances the loveliest inspirations to great thoughts—all first fruits are delicious. In grown men, love becomes an obsession, and strength leads to abuse. In dotards it becomes vice, and impotence leads to extremes. Now Henri was at once a dotard, a grown man, and a youth. For him to feel the emotions of true love, he needed, like Lovelace, a Clarissa Harlowe. Without the magical gleam of that unattainable pearl, he was capable of nothing but passions piqued by some Parisian vanity, or some wager with himself to corrupt a certain woman, or escapades that aroused his curiosity. The report conveyed by Laurent, his personal valet, had enormously increased the value of the *girl with the golden eyes*. He would have to do battle with a secret enemy who seemed to be as dangerous as he was cunning; and to emerge victorious, Henri would have to call upon all the forces at his command. He was about to act out that eternally old but ever new comedy featuring the stock characters of an old man, a young girl, and a lover: Don Hijos, Paquita, and de Marsay. Laurent was prepared to play the role of Figaro, but the duenna seemed incorruptible. So this real-life drama was more complicated by chance than it had ever been by any author writing for the stage! But after all, chance has its own genius.

This will take careful planning, Henri said to himself.

"Well," said Paul de Manerville as he came in, "How are things? I've come to have lunch with you."

"Fine," said Henri. "You won't be shocked if I go on dressing while you're here?"

"You're joking!"

"We take so much from the English at the moment that we are in danger of becoming hypocrites and prudes like them," Henri said.

Laurent had brought his master so many elaborate and charming things to choose from that Paul could not help remarking: "But won't this take you two hours?"

"No," Henri replied, "two and a half."

"Well, since we're alone and can speak openly, tell me why a superior man like you, and you are superior, should affect a foppishness that is not natural to him. Why spend two and a half hours grooming yourself when in fifteen minutes you can bathe,

55

quickly brush your hair, and put your clothes on? Why go to all this trouble?"

"I must be very fond of you, you big oaf, to confide such lofty thoughts," said the young man who at that moment was having his feet brushed with a soft brush rubbed with English soap.

"But I am sincerely devoted to you," Paul de Manerville replied, "and I'm fond of you because I understand you are superior to me . . ."

"You must have noticed, if you're capable of observing a moral truth, that women love fops," de Marsay replied, without responding to Paul's declaration with more than a glance. "Do you know why women love fops? My friend, fops are the only men who look after themselves. Now, isn't looking after oneself too assiduously only a way of looking after what belongs to another? The man who does not belong to himself is the very man women are fond of, since love is essentially a thief.

"I'm not referring to that excessive cleanliness they adore. Yet I challenge you to find one of them who has a passion for a slovenly man, as remarkable as he may be. If such a thing has happened, we must chalk it up to a pregnant woman's whims, to those silly ideas that float through anyone's mind. On the other hand, I have seen truly remarkable men left flat because of their negligence. A fop concerned only with his person is preoccupied with nonsense and trivial things. And what is woman? A trivial thing, a bundle of nonsense. Toss off a few good witticisms and you can keep her busy for hours. She's sure the fop will pay attention to her, since he has nothing better to do. He will never neglect her for glory, ambition, politics, or art, those great public courtesans she considers her rivals. And fops have the courage to incur ridicule to please a woman, whose heart goes out to the man who makes a fool of himself for love. Indeed, a fop can be a fop only if he has earned it. And only women can confer that dignity. The fop is love's colonel, he earns his victories with a regiment of women at his command!

"My dear fellow, in Paris there are no secrets, and a man cannot be a fop here free of charge. You, for instance, have only one woman—and perhaps you're right. But try playing the fop: You'd not only make a fool of yourself, you'd be dead. You'd become a walking prejudice, one of those men condemned to do the same old thing over and over. You'd stand for *stupidity* the way Monsieur de Lafayette stands for America, Monsieur de Tallyrand for diplomacy, Desaugiers for singing, and Monsieur de Segur for musical theater. Let them stray from their speciality and no one would value what they do. That's how we are in France, always supremely unjust! Monsieur de Tal-

lyrand could be a great financier, Monsieur de Lafayette a tyrant, and Desaugiers an administrator.
You might have forty women next year, but no one
would credit you publicly with a single one.

"So Paul, my friend, foppishness is the sign of un-
questionable power over the female population. A
man loved by several women is thought to have superior qualities; and then it's only a question of who
will grab him, poor man! But don't disparage the
right to enter a drawing room, look around at everyone from the height of your cravat or through your
monocle, and feel contempt for the most outstanding
man because his waistcoat is unfashionable. Laurent,
you're hurting me! After lunch, Paul, we shall go to
the Tuileries and see the adorable *girl with the golden
eyes.*"

After an excellent meal, the two young men
strolled on the terrace of Feuillant's and along the
main path of the Tuileries but found no trace of the
sublime Paquita Valdes, for whose sake fifty of the
most elegant young men in Paris, all of them perfumed and cravated to their chins, booted, spurred,
and cracking their whips, were walking, talking,
laughing, and generally boistrous.

"Nil," said Henri. "But I've just had a marvelous
idea. That girl receives letters from London; we must
bribe the postman or get him tipsy, open a letter, read

it of course, slip in a little billet-doux, and seal it up again. The old tyrant, *crudel tiranno*, must surely know the woman who writes the letters coming from London and would suspect nothing."

The next day de Marsay came again to stroll in the sun on the terrace of Feuillant's and there he saw Paquita Valdes, already enhanced by the passion he felt for her. He was mad about those eyes flashing like the rays of the sun, their ardor mirrored by that perfect, voluptuous body. De Marsay was burning to brush against the dress of that charming girl as they strolled past each other, but his attempts were always thwarted. Once when he had overtaken the duenna and Paquita, and was about to turn around so as to walk beside the *girl with the golden eyes*, Paquita, no less impatient, hurried forward and de Marsay felt her squeeze his hand so quickly and passionately, he thought he had felt the jolt of an electric shock. Instantly all the emotions of youth surged into his heart. When the lovers' eyes met, Paquita seemed ashamed; she lowered her eyes to avoid Henri's, but nonetheless stole a glance at the feet and figure of the man she would have called, as women did before the Revolution, her *conqueror*.

I will certainly make this girl my mistress, Henri said to himself.

Following her to the end of the terrace in the direction of Place Louis XV, he noticed the old Marquis de San-Réal walking on the arm of his valet, stepping carefully like a dyspeptic suffering from gout. Doña Concha, who mistrusted Henri, kept Paquita between herself and the old gentleman.

And as for you! de Marsay said to himself, glancing contemptuously at the duenna, if we can't make you cooperate, we'll put you to sleep with a little opium. We know our mythology and the story of Argus.

Before climbing into her carriage, the *girl with the golden eyes* exchanged a few unambiguous glances with her lover, and Henri was enchanted. But the duenna intercepted one of them and spoke sharply to Paquita, who threw herself into the carriage in evident desperation. For several days Paquita did not come to the Tuileries. Laurent, who was posted as lookout at the mansion on his master's orders, learned from the neighbors that neither the two women nor the old Marquis had gone out since the day the duenna had intercepted a glance between Henri and the young lady entrusted to her care. So the delicate bond that had united the two lovers was already broken.

Several days later, no one knows how, de Marsay achieved his goal. He had a seal and sealing wax absolutely identical to those used on the letters sent from London to Mademoiselle Valdes, paper similar to the paper used by her London correspondent, and all the tools needed for imprinting English and French postmarks. He had written the following letter, which he embellished with all the marks of a letter sent from London.

"Dear Paquita,

I will not try to describe in words the passion you have inspired in me. If, to my great joy, you share it, please know that I have found the means to correspond with you. My name is Adolphe de Gouges, and I live at 54 Rue de l'Université. Your silence will tell me whether you are too closely watched to write or have no paper or pens. So if you have not thrown a letter over the wall of your garden into the Baron de Nucingen's, where someone will be waiting to-morrow between eight in the morning and ten in the evening, then a man who is my devoted servant will slip you two vials on the end of a cord. One will contain opium to put your Argus to sleep—six drops will be enough. The other will contain ink. The vial of ink is of cut glass, the other is smooth. Both are flat enough for you to hide in your corset. All I have done to send you this letter must tell you how much I love you. If you doubt it, I swear to you that I would give my life for one hour with you."

They always believe that sort of thing, poor creatures! de Marsay said to himself. But they're right. What would we think of a woman who refused to be seduced by such a convincing love letter?

The following day at around eight o'clock in the morning, this letter was delivered by good Sparo, the postman, to the concierge of the San-Réal mansion.

In order to be near the field of battle, de Marsay had come to lunch with Paul, who lived in Rue de la Pepinière. At two o'clock, just as the two friends were laughing over the downfall of a young man who had tried to lead an elegant life without the requisite fortune and wondering how he would fare, Henri's coachman came to find his master at Paul's and introduced him to a mysterious person who insisted on speaking to him alone. This person was a mulatto who would surely have inspired Talma to play Othello, had he chanced to meet him. Never did an African face more openly express the magnitude of revenge, the swiftness of suspicion, the immediate translation of thought into action, the strength of the Moor and his childish impetuosity. His black eyes stared like the eyes of a bird of prey, and they were encased like the eyes of a vulture in a bluish membrane devoid of lashes. His low, narrow forehead looked menacing. This man was obviously driven by a single thought. His sinewed arm was at another's command.

He was followed by a man whom every imagination, whether shivering in Greenland or sweltering in New England, would describe as a *wretched fellow*. By this phrase everyone will represent him according to his own familiar ideas. But who can imagine his pale face, wrinkled and reddish around the edges, and his long beard? Who can picture his discolored, stringy cravat, his greasy shirt collar, his shabby hat, his shiny frock coat, his pitiful trousers, his shrunken waistcoat, his imitation gold tie pin, his dirt-encrusted shoes and muddy laces? Who can comprehend the vastness of his past and present poverty? Only a Parisian. The wretched man in Paris is utterly wretched, for he still finds enough joy to know just how wretched he is. The mulatto seemed to be one of Louis XI's executioners leading a man to the gallows.

"Where did these two rascals come from?" said Henri.

"Good God!" Paul replied. "One of them gives me the shivers."

"Who are you?" Henri said, looking at the wretched fellow. "You seem more of a Christian than this other one."

The mulatto kept his eyes fixed on the two young men, like a deaf man trying to read their gestures and the movements of their lips.

"I'm a public scribe and interpreter. I'm from the Palais de Justice and my name is Poincet."

"Fine. And what about this one?" Henri said to Poincet, indicating the mulatto.

"I don't know. He speaks only a kind of Spanish dialect and brought me here to help you reach some agreement."

The mulatto drew from his pocket the letter Henri had written to Paquita and returned it to him; Henri threw it in the fire.

Well, things are beginning to shape up, Henri said to himself. "Paul, leave us alone a moment."

"I have translated that letter for him," continued the interpreter when they were alone. "When it was translated he went off somewhere. Then he came looking for me again to bring me here, promising me two louis."

"What do you have to tell me, Chinaman?" Henri asked.

"I left out *Chinaman*," said the interpreter while waiting for the mulatto's reply.

"He says, sir," continued the interpreter after listening to the stranger, "that tomorrow evening at half past ten you must wait on Boulevard Montmartre, near the café. You will see a carriage and you will climb in, saying to the person opening the door: *cortejo*—a Spanish word that means *lover*," added Poincet, with a glance of congratulations at Henri.

"Good!"

The mulatto wanted to pay the man two louis, but de Marsay would not allow it and rewarded the interpreter himself. While he was paying him, the mulatto spoke several words.

"What did he say?"

"He's warning me," replied the poor man, "that if I commit a single indiscretion, he'll strangle me. He's a fine one and looks quite capable of it."

"I'm sure of that," answered Henri. "He would do as he says."

"He adds," continued the interpreter, "that the woman who sent him begs you, for your own sake and for hers, to exercise the greatest caution because the daggers held over your heads would pierce your hearts, and no human power could save you."

"He said that! So much the better, this will be even more entertaining. You can come back in, Paul!" he called to his friend.

The mulatto, who had continued to stare at the

lover of Paquita Valdes with riveted attention, took his leave, followed by the interpreter.

"At last, here's a truly romantic adventure," Henri said when Paul returned. "After taking part in a few Parisian intrigues, I've finally found one that involves serious circumstances and grave danger. Damn it! how danger plucks up a woman's courage! Tormenting a woman and trying to thwart her gives her the right and the heart to leap over obstacles that would have taken her years to overcome. Go, dear creature, take the leap. 'Dying'? Poor child! 'Daggers'? Women have such imaginations! They all need to dramatize their little pranks. Anyway, we'll think it over, Paquita! We'll think it over, my girl! The devil take me, now that I know this beautiful girl, this masterpiece of nature is mine, the adventure is not quite so delicious."

Despite these superficial words, the young man in Henri had reappeared. In order to dull the distress of waiting until the next evening, he took refuge in exorbitant pleasures: He played cards, dined with his friends; he drank like a coachman, ate like a German, and won ten or twelve thousand francs. He left the famous restaurant Rocher de Cancale at two in the morning, slept like a baby, awoke fresh and rosy the next day, and dressed to go to the Tuileries, planning to see Paquita, ride horseback to work up an appetite, and have a good dinner—all this to kill time.

At the appointed hour Henri was on the boulevard, spied the carriage, and gave the password to a man he took to be the mulatto. At this signal the man opened the door and quickly unfolded the steps. Henri was driven through Paris so swiftly, and his thoughts left him so little capacity to observe the streets he was passing through, that he had no idea where the carriage stopped. The mulatto led him into a house with a staircase very near the coach entrance. This staircase was as gloomy as the landing where Henri was forced to wait while the mulatto went to open the door to a dank, airless, ill-lit apartment, whose rooms, illuminated only by the candle his guide had found in the foyer, seemed empty and inadequately furnished, like the rooms of a house whose inhabitants are off traveling. He recognized the sensation he felt when reading the novels of Ann Radcliffe, in which the hero makes his way through the cold, gloomy halls of some melancholy and deserted place. At last the mulatto opened the door to a salon. The condition of the old furniture and faded hangings that decorated this room made it look like the salon of a brothel. There was the same pretense of elegance and the same clutter of vulgar trinkets, the same dust and squalor. On a couch covered with red Utrecht velvet, beside a smoldering hearth, sat an old, rather shabbily dressed woman wearing one of those turbans contrived by English women when they reach a certain age and admired no end in China, where monstrosity is the artist's ideal. This salon, this old woman, this cold hearth might have chilled his love if Paquita had not been there on a love seat in a voluptuous peignoir, free to flash her golden glance, free to exhibit her beautifully arched foot, free in her luminous movements.

This first interview was like all first meetings between passionate people who have swiftly crossed distances full of ardent desire before they really know each other. They are bound to find something discordant in the situation, which is embarrassing until the moment when their souls become attuned. If desire emboldens a man and makes him press forward, holding nothing back, his mistress, no matter how deeply she is in love, is afraid of arriving at the goal too soon and facing the necessity of surrender, which for most women amounts to a fall into an abyss where they have no idea what they will find. The woman's involuntary coldness is in sharp contrast to the man's avowed passion, and necessarily affects the most smitten lover. These ideas, which often float like vapors around their souls, afflict them with a kind of temporary malady. In the sweet journey two creatures undertake through the blissful lands of love, this moment is like a heath that must be crossed, a deserted heath, by turns humid and hot, full of swamps and burning sands. Yet this leads to the laughing, rose-hung groves where love and his retinue of pleasures gambol on the finely covered green. Often the intelligent man finds that a foolish laugh is the only useful response to all this; his mind is, as it were, numbed by the glacial compression of his desires. It is even possible that two such beautiful, intelligent, and passionate creatures might at first utter the most idiotic commonplaces, until a chance word, a tremulous glance, a spark ignited conveys them through the happy transition that leads them down the flower-strewn path where they do not walk but glide.

This state of the soul is always in proportion to the violence of one's feelings. Two creatures whose love is halfhearted have no such experience. The effect of this crisis may further be compared to the effect of heat in a cloudless sky. At first glance nature seems covered by a gauzy veil, the blue of the heavens seems black, the light is so intense it resembles darkness. Both Henri and the Spanish girl encountered in themselves a similar violence; and the law of statics, which rules that when two identical forces meet they cancel each other out, might be true in the psychological realm as well.

And the embarrassment of this moment was singularly increased by the presence of the old mummy. Love is inhibited or encouraged by all sorts of things; everything is construed as significant, an omen of happiness or doom. This decrepit woman was there as a possible conclusion to their story, embodying the hideous fishtail which the symbol-making geniuses of Greece attributed to their Chimeras and Sirens, so enchanting and deceptive above the waist—like all budding passions. Although Henri was not a rationalist—this word is always a mockery—but a man of extraordinary power, a man as great as a nonbeliever can be, the convergence of all these circumstances impressed him enormously. Besides, the strongest men are naturally the most impressionable, and therefore the most superstitious, if one can call superstition the prejudice of a first impulse, which is no doubt an intuition of the effects of causes hidden from other eyes but perceptible to theirs.

The Spanish girl took advantage of this momentary stupor to surrender to the ecstasy of that infinite adoration which seizes a woman's heart when she truly loves and finds herself in the presence of an idol she has longed for in vain. Her eyes sparkled, full of joy and happiness. She was under a spell and fearlessly intoxicated with long imagined happiness. She seemed so enchantingly beautiful to Henri that the whole phantasmagoria of rags, old age, worn red draperies, and green straw mats in front of armchairs, unpolished red tiles, and all this sickly and ailing luxury soon vanished. The salon was illuminated, and it was only through the hazy light that he glimpsed the terrible harpie, stiff and mute on her red couch, her yellow eyes betraying the servile attitude inspired by misfortune or by some enslaving vice that acts like a brutal tyrant with his despotic lashings. Her eyes had the cold flash of those of a caged tiger, who understands his impotence and is forced to swallow his own desire to destroy.

"Who is this woman?" Henri said to Paquita.

But Paquita did not reply. She signaled that she did not understand French and asked Henri if he spoke English. De Marsay repeated his question in English.

"She's the only woman I can trust, although she sold me once already," said Paquita calmly. "My dear Adolphe, she's my mother, a slave bought in Georgia for her rare beauty, though not much of it is left. She speaks only her native tongue."

This woman's attitude and her desire to understand by their gestures what was going on between her daughter and Henri suddenly became clear to the young man, and this explanation put him at his ease.

"Paquita," he said to her, "shall we not be free, then?"

"Never!" she said sadly. "We have only a few days together."

She looked down at her hand and counted with her right hand the fingers of her left, displaying the most beautiful hands Henri had ever seen.

"One, two three . . ."

She counted to twelve.

"Yes," she said, "we have twelve days."

"And after that?"

"After that," she said, with the distracted air of a woman under the executioner's ax and slain in advance by a fear that stripped her of the magnificent energy nature seemed to have endowed her with in order to intensify sensual delight and convert the crudest pleasures into endless poetry.

"After that," she repeated. Her eyes became fixed; she seemed to contemplate some distant, menacing object. "I don't know," she said.

This girl is mad, thought Henri, surrendering to strange reflections.

Paquita seemed preoccupied with something other than him, like a woman torn between passion and remorse. Perhaps she had another love in her heart that she was remembering and forgetting by turns. In an instant Henri was assailed by a thousand contradictory thoughts. This girl became a mystery to him; but appraising her with the expert attention of the jaded man starved for novel delights, like an Oriental potentate always after new pleasures—a terrible thirst that comes upon great souls—Henri recognized in Paquita the richest organization nature was pleased to create for love. The supposed action of this mechanism, leaving aside any question of the soul, would have frightened another man. But de Marsay was fascinated by that rich harvest of promised pleasures, by that constantly varied happiness which is every man's dream and the goal of every woman in love. He was driven wild by the infinite made palpable and transported to the most extreme raptures the human creature can know. He saw all that in this girl more clearly than ever before, for she surrendered complacently to his gaze, happy to be admired. De Marsay's admiration became a hidden frenzy, and he conveyed it all to her in a look which the Spanish girl understood, as if she were accustomed to being looked at in this way.

"If you cannot be mine alone, I would kill you!" he cried.

Hearing this, Paquita hid her face in her hands and

cried naively: "Holy Virgin, have I fallen into a trap?"

She rose, threw herself on the red couch, plunged her head into the rags covering her mother's breast, and wept. The old woman received her daughter without moving, without registering any emotion. The mother was in supreme possession of that gravity of savage peoples, that stony impassivity which defies scrutiny. Did she love her daughter or didn't she? No reply. Beneath that mask smoldered all human feelings, good and bad, and anything might be expected from this creature. Her gaze moved slowly from her daughter's beautiful hair, which covered her like a mantilla, to Henri's face, which she examined with inexpressible curiosity. She seemed to be wondering what enchantment had brought him there, and what caprice of nature had created such a captivating man.

These women are toying with me! Henri said to himself.

Just then Paquita raised her head and threw him one of those burning looks that penetrate to the very soul. She seemed so lovely that he vowed this treasure of beauty should belong to him.

"My Paquita, be mine!"

"But you want to kill me?" she said in a frightened, quivering, anxious voice, drawn to him nonetheless by an inexplicable force.

"Kill you? I?" he said smiling.

Paquita gave a startled cry, spoke a word to the old woman, who regally took Henri's hand and that of her daughter, gave them a long look, then released them with a dreadful and significant nod.

"Be mine this evening, this very moment! Come with me, don't leave me! I want you, Paquita! Do you love me? Then come!"

In an instant he spoke a thousand senseless things to her with the swiftness of a flood that rushes over rocks, repeating the same sound in a thousand different forms.

It's the same voice, Paquita whispered wistfully to herself, and the same passion.

"Oh yes!" she said, with passionate abandon. "Yes, but not this evening. This evening, Adolphe, I have given la Concha too little opium. She might wake up and I would be lost. At this very moment the whole house thinks I'm asleep in my room. Be at the same place in two days, give the same man the same password. This man is my foster father; Christemio adores me and would die of torture rather than utter a word against me. Adieu," she said, clinging to Henri and wrapping herself around him like a serpent.

She pressed herself against him, raised her head to his, offered him her lips, and gave him a kiss that made them both swoon so that de Marsay thought the earth would open before him, and Paquita cried: "Go!" in a voice that betrayed how little she was mistress of herself. But she clung to him, still crying: "Go!" and led him slowly to the stairs.

There the mulatto, whose white eyes gleamed at the sight of Paquita, took the torch from the hands of his idol and led Henri to the street. He left the torch under the vault, opened the door, put Henri back into the carriage, and with marvelous swiftness deposited him on the Boulevard des Italiens. The horses seemed to be driven by hell's own fury.

To de Marsay this scene was like a dream, but one of those dreams which, in vanishing, leaves the soul with a feeling of such supernatural delight that a man might pursue it the rest of his days. A single kiss had been enough. No rendezvous had taken place in such a proper, chaste, even chill fashion, in more dreadful surroundings, or in the presence of a more hideous divinity. For the mother lingered on in Henri's imagination like something infernal, crouching, cadaverous, vicious, savagely ferocious, something not yet limned in the fantasy of poets and painters. Indeed, no rendezvous had so stimulated his senses, revealed more daring delights, or made desire surge so powerfully from the center of his being and spread like an aura around him. There was something dark, mysterious, sweet and tender, constrained and expansive, a coupling of the horrible and the heavenly, of hell and paradise, that made de Marsay drunk. He was no longer himself, yet he still had strength enough to resist the intoxications of pleasure.

To understand his behavior at the conclusion to this story, it must be explained that his soul had expanded at the age when most young men diminish themselves by mingling with women and becoming too obsessed with them. He had grown by a convergence of secret circumstances that endowed him with vast, hidden power. This young man had a scepter mightier than those held by modern kings, whose slightest whims are nearly all reined in by the law. De Marsay exercised the autocratic power of an Oriental despot. But this power, so stupidly wielded in Asia by brutal men, was matched by European intelligence and French wit, which is the keenest and sharpest of intellectual instruments. Henri could do whatever he wanted to satisfy his pleasures and vanities. This invisible influence on the social world had clothed him in a real but secret majesty, a majesty that was not flaunted but veiled. His view of himself was not that of Louis XIV but that of the proudest caliphs, of the pharoahs who believed they were scions of a divine race when they imitated God by concealing themselves from their subjects under the pretext that their gaze was fatal.

So, unrepentant in his role as both judge and jury, de Marsay coldly condemned to death any man or woman who seriously offended him. Although often pronounced rather lightly, the verdict was irrevocable. Any error was a disaster of the sort caused when lightning strikes some happy Parisian woman setting out in a cab, instead of felling the old coachman taking her to a rendezvous. And the acerbic, probing irony that distinguished this young man's conversation rather generally spread alarm: No one felt inclined to argue with him. Women are prodigiously fond of these men who regard themselves as pashas, who seem to trail a retinue of lions and executioners, and spread terror around them as they go. Such men exude self-assurance in their actions, confidence in their power, with an arrogant gaze and a leonine presence that embodies the type of strength all women dream of. Such was de Marsay.

Now he was happy in anticipation of the future; he became young and pliable, and upon retiring to his bed thought only of love. He dreamed, as passionate young men dream, of the *girl with the golden eyes*. Dreams full of monstrous, evanescent, and bizarre images, full of light, revealed invisible worlds that were nonetheless incomplete, for an interposing veil distorted his view. The next day and the day after he disappeared, telling no one where he had gone. His potency belonged to him only under certain conditions, and fortunately for him during these two days he was a foot soldier in the service of the demon from which he held his talismanic existence. But at the appointed hour that evening, he waited on the boulevard for the carriage, which was not long in coming. The mulatto approached Henri and repeated to him in French a sentence he seemed to have learned by heart:

"If you want to come, she told me, you must agree to be blindfolded."

And Christemio produced a white silk scarf.

"No!" said Henri, whose power suddenly asserted itself.

And he tried to climb into the carriage. The mulatto made a sign; the carriage pulled away.

"Yes!" cried de Marsay, enraged at the possibility of losing the pleasure he had promised himself. Besides, he saw the impossibility of negotiating with a slave who was as blindly obedient as an executioner. Furthermore, why should his anger be aimed at this passive instrument?

The mulatto whistled and the carriage returned. Henri quickly climbed in. Several curious passersby had already gathered on the boulevard to gawk. Henri was strong and decided to stand up to the mulatto. When the carriage set off at a fast trot, he grabbed the man's hands in order to subdue his guardian and preserve the use of his own faculties to discover where he was going. A useless effort. The mulatto's eyes glittered in the dark. The man gave a furious shout, wrenched free, pushed de Marsay away with one iron hand and nailed him, as it were, to the floor of the carriage. Then with his free hand he drew a triangular dagger and whistled again. The coachman heard the whistle and stopped. Henri had no weapon and was forced to yield; he held his head out toward the scarf. This gesture of submission appeased Christemio, who blindfolded him with a respect and care that bore witness to his veneration for the person of the man his idol loved. But having taken this precaution, he squeezed his dagger warily into his side pocket and buttoned himself up to the chin.

That Chinaman would have killed me! de Marsay said to himself.

The carriage once more rolled swiftly on. There was one last resource for a young man who knew Paris as well as Henri did. He might have discovered his destination had he simply composed himself and counted the number of gutters that marked the streets they were crossing on the boulevards as the carriage continued on its way. He might have recognized whether the carriage was turning off toward the Seine or toward the heights of Montmartre, and determined the name or position of the street where his guide would stop the carriage. But the violent emotion caused by his struggle, his rage at compromising his dignity, the thoughts of vengeance to which he surrendered, the speculations prompted by the extreme precautions this mysterious girl had taken to bring him to her—all prevented him from focusing that blind man's attention necessary to the concentration of mind and the accuracy of memory.

The journey lasted half an hour. When the carriage stopped, it was no longer on the pavement. The mulatto and the coachman took Henri in their arms, lifted him up, put him on a kind of litter, and carried him through a garden where he smelled the flowers and the distinctive scent of the trees and shrubs. The surrounding silence was so pervasive, he could hear the sound of water dripping from the damp leaves. The two men took him up a staircase, set him on his feet, led him by the hand through several rooms, and left him in a room redolent of perfume where he felt a thick carpet underfoot. A feminine hand pushed him down on a couch and removed the scarf. Henri saw Paquita standing before him, but it was Paquita in all her sensual glory.

The part of the boudoir in which Henri found himself formed a graceful circular line, in contrast to the other part, which was perfectly square and framed a gleaming fireplace of white and gilt marble. He had entered by a side door hidden behind a rich tapestry curtain facing a window. The horseshoe portion of the room was furnished with a real Turkish divan, a mattress as wide as a bed fifty feet in circumference, placed directly on the floor and covered in white cashmere with a lozenge pattern of flaming red and black silk rosettes. The backing of this vast bed rose several inches above the numerous cushions that graced it with their harmonious charm.

This boudoir was draped in a red fabric hung with Indian muslin fluted like a Corinthian column in alternating folds, and bordered at the top and bottom with a band of flame red fabric worked with black arabesques. Beneath the muslin the red was softened to pink, a romantic color echoed by the window curtains of Indian muslin lined with pink taffeta and decorated with red and black fringe. Six silver sconces, each holding two candles, were attached to the wall coverings at equal distances to illuminate the divan. The ceiling, graced by a central chandelier of matte silver, was dazzlingly white with a gilt cornice. The carpet was like an Oriental shawl and recalled the poetry of Persia, where it had been worked by the hands of slaves. The furnishings were covered in white cashmere enhanced by black and flame red. The clock, the candelabras, everything was in white and gilt marble. The only table in the room was covered with a cashmere throw. Elegant vases contained roses of all kinds, and red or white flowers. Indeed, the smallest detail seemed to have been chosen with loving care.

Never had wealth been more artfully disguised to express elegance and grace, and to inspire lust. The coldest creature would have warmed to this setting. The iridescent hangings, whose color changed from different angles, now white, now all pink, blended with the effects of the light that infused the diaphanous flutings of the muslin, producing gauzy apparitions. The soul has some mysterious attachment to white, love revels in red, and gold enflames the passions with its power to make their fantasies come true. All man's vague and mysterious aspects, all his unexplained affinities, were soothed here in their involuntary sympathies. In this perfect harmony there was a concert of colors to which the soul responded with sensual, imprecise, elusive ideas.

In the midst of this heady atmosphere laden with exquisite perfumes, Paquita appeared to Henri dressed in a white peignoir, barefoot, with orange blossoms in her black hair. She was kneeling before him, worshipping him like the god of this temple he had deigned to visit. Although de Marsay was used to the refinements of Parisian luxury, he was surprised at the sight of this shell-like chamber, so like the birthplace of Venus. Whether it was the contrast between the darkness from which he had emerged and the light that bathed his soul, or a quick comparison between this scene and the setting of their first conversation, he experienced one of those delicate sensations that inspire true poetry. When, in this alcove conjured by a fairy's wand, Henri glimpsed this masterpiece of creation, this girl with the warm coloring whose soft skin was lightly burnished by reddish reflections and the hidden emanations of love, glistening as if reflecting rays of color and light, his anger, his desires for vengeance, his wounded vanity all evaporated. Like an eagle swooping on his prey, he took her in his arms, seated her on his knees, and was indescribably intoxicated by the sensual pressure of this girl, whose amply developed charms softly enveloped him.

"Come, Paquita!" he said in a low voice.

"Speak! Speak without fear," she said to him. "This refuge was made for love. No sound can escape, so solidly was it built to protect the accents and music of the beloved voice. Cry out as loudly as you like, nothing can be heard beyond this chamber. Someone could be murdered here, but the victim might as well be screaming in the Sahara."

"Who has understood jealousy and its needs so well?"

"Never question me about such things," she replied, undoing the young man's cravat with infinitely gentle fingers, doubtless to get a better view of his graceful neck.

"Yes, there's that neck I love so much!" she said. "Do you want to please me?"

This question, asked almost lewdly, drew de Marsay from the musings in which he was plunged by Paquita's despotic reply forbidding any inquiry into the unknown being who hovered over them like a shadow.

"And if I wanted to know who rules here?"

Paquita trembled as she gazed at him.

"It's certainly not me, then," he said, rising and releasing this girl, who fell back. "Wherever I am, I want to stand alone."

"Go ahead! Kill me!" said the poor slave girl, terrified.

"Who do you take me for? Answer me!"

Paquita rose humbly, her eyes full of tears, took a dagger from one of the two ebony chests, and offered it to Henri with a gesture of submission that would have soothed a tiger's fury.

"Delight me as men do when they love," she said, "and while I'm asleep, kill me, for I could never answer you. Listen: I'm chained like a poor animal to its post; I'm amazed I've been able to throw a bridge across the abyss that divides us. Make me drunk, then kill me. Oh, no, no!" she said, joining her hands, "do not kill me! I love life! Life is so beautiful to me! If I am a slave, I am also a queen. I could deceive you with words, tell you that I love only you, prove it to you, and take advantage of my momentary sway to tell you: 'Take me the way one savors the scent of a flower in a king's garden.' Then, after using a woman's eloquent guile and spreading the wings of pleasure, after quenching my thirst, I could have you thrown into a well where no one would find you, a well built to satisfy vengeance without fear of justice, a well full of quicklime to be set on fire so that not a shred of your being remained. You would stay in my heart, mine forever."

Henri looked at this girl without trembling, and his fearless gaze made her flush with joy.

"No, I won't do it! You did not fall into a trap here, but into the heart of a woman who adores you, and I'm the one who will be thrown into the well."

"All this seems awfully strange to me," de Marsay said, examining her closely. "Yet despite your bizarre nature you seem to be a good-hearted girl; upon my word, I cannot make heads or tails of you or find the right word to describe you."

Paquita had no idea what the young man meant. She looked at him sweetly, but not stupidly, widening her eyes, which were filled with such depths of sensuality.

"Tell me, my love," she said, coming back to her first thought, "do you want to please me?"

"I'll do whatever you want and even what you don't want," de Marsay laughingly replied, recovering his foppish nonchalance and resolving to accept his good fortune without looking back or too far ahead. And perhaps he was counting on his power and on his experience as a man of the world to dominate this girl in a few hours' time and learn all her secrets.

"Well," she said to him, "let me dress you as I like."

"By all means, dress me as you like," Henri said.

Paquita joyfully took a red velvet dress from one of the chests and slipped it on de Marsay, then she crowned him with a woman's hat and wrapped him in a shawl. Yielding to her whims with the innocence of a child, she was convulsed with laughter, like a bird beating its wings. But she saw nothing more.

While it may be impossible to describe the unexpected delights enjoyed by these two beautiful creatures invented in a moment of heavenly joy, it seems appropriate to translate metaphysically the young man's extraordinary, almost fantastical impressions. People who find themselves in de Marsay's social position and live as he lived are above all capable of recognizing a girl's innocence. The strangest thing was, however, that although the *girl with the golden eyes* was a virgin, she was certainly not innocent. The bizarre union of mystery and reality, of light and shadow, of horror and beauty, of pleasure and fear, of heaven and hell already encountered in this adventure extended to the capricious and sublime being with whom de Marsay dallied. The most esoteric refinements of sensuality, all Henri could have known of that poetry of the senses called love, was surpassed by the treasures proffered by this girl, true to the promise of her flashing eyes. She was an Oriental poem radiant with the sun that Sa'di and Hafez infused into their vaulting verse. But neither Sa'di's rhythm nor Pindar's would have expressed the delirious, dazed ecstasy that gripped this delicious girl when her delusion, guided by an iron hand, finally ceased.

"Dead!" she said, "I am dead! Adolphe, take me to the ends of the earth, to an island where no one knows us. Our flight must leave no trace! We shall be followed even to hell. My God! It's dawn. Save yourself. Will I ever see you again? Yes, I must see you again tomorrow, even if I have to kill all my keepers. Until tomorrow."

She threw her arms around him in an embrace that

made him fear for his life. Then she pushed a button that must have activated a bell, and begged de Marsay to let her blindfold him.

"And what if I've changed my mind, what if I wanted to stay?"

"You would only hasten my death," she said, "for now I'm sure I shall die for you."

Henri allowed himself to be blindfolded.

The man who has just gorged himself on pleasure is inclined to forgetfulness, a kind of ingratitude, a desire for freedom, a desire to go for a stroll; he feels a hint of contempt and perhaps disgust for his idol; indeed, he experiences certain incomprehensible feelings that make him malicious. No doubt the understanding of this vague but genuine emotion in souls neither bathed by the celestial light nor perfumed by the sacred balm that allows us to sustain our feelings prompted Rousseau to relate the adventures of Lord Edward in the final letters of *La Nouvelle Héloise*. Rousseau was clearly inspired by the work of Richardson, but he differed from Richardson in a thousand details that make his masterpiece magnificently original. His profound ideas, so admired by posterity, are difficult to distinguish when one reads this work in one's youth for the sake of its warm depiction of our most physical feelings, while serious writers and philosophers never allude to it except as the corollary or consequence of a vast system of thought. And Lord Edward's adventures express the most quintessentially European ideas with great delicacy.

Henri was, then, in the grip of that ambiguous feeling incompatible with real love. In some sense he needed the flow of comparisons to cease and the irresistible pull of recollections to lead him back to a woman. True love triumphs above all through memory. Can a woman ever be loved who has not left a lasting impression in a man's soul, either by sating him with pleasure or by overwhelming him with the strength of her feelings? Unbeknown to Henri, Paquita had taken hold within him by both means. But just now, overcome by the fatigue of happiness, that delicious physical melancholy, he could hardly analyze his heart by recalling the taste of the most vivid sensual pleasures he had ever known.

He found himself on Boulevard Montmartre at dawn, staring stupidly after the departing carriage. He took two cigars from his pocket and lit one at the lantern of a good woman who was selling brandy and coffee to workers, street urchins, and market gardeners, all those Parisians who start their lives before daybreak. Then he strolled off, smoking his cigar, thrusting his hands in his trouser pockets with a truly disgraceful nonchalance.

Ah, there's nothing like a cigar! Something a man never tires of, he said to himself.

He had hardly a thought for that *girl with the golden eyes* who was the toast of all the elegant young men of Paris at the time. The idea of death expressed through sensual pleasures, the fear of which had several times darkened the brow of this beautiful creature—connected to the houris of Asia through her mother, to Europe through her education, to the Tropics through her birth—seemed to him one of those impostures by which all women try to make themselves interesting.

"She's from Havana, Capital of the most Spanish country in the New World; so she mimics terror rather than confronting me with anguish, complications, coyness, or duty as Parisian ladies do. By her golden eyes, I have the greatest wish to sleep."

He saw a cab for hire standing at the corner of Frascati's, waiting to pick up gamblers. He woke the driver, hired him to drive him home, went to bed, and slept the sleep of the damned, which, by a bizarre coincidence that no song writer has yet recorded, is as deep as that of innocence. Perhaps this is an example of the maxim: *Les extrèmes se touchent.*

Toward noon de Marsay stretched his arms as he awoke, and felt the pangs of one of those ravenous hungers which all old soldiers can remember feeling the day after a victory. And he was pleased to see Paul de Manerville make his entrance, for nothing is more agreeable in such circumstances than eating in company.

"Well," Paul said to his friend, "we were all imagining that for the past ten days you've been shut up with the *girl with the golden eyes*."

"The *girl with the golden eyes*! I haven't given her a thought. Good Lord! I have other fish to fry."

"Ah, you're being discreet!"

"Why not?" de Marsay said, laughing. "My dear fellow, discretion is is the better part of valor—and more profitable besides. Listen . . . No, I won't say a word. You won't learn a thing from me, I'm not inclined to give away the gems of my strategy for nothing. Life is a flow of commercial exchange. I swear by all I hold most sacred—by cigars—that I'm not a professor of social economy at the disposal of ninnies. Let's eat. It costs less to give you a tuna omelette than to waste my brains on you."

"So you keep accounts with your friends?"

"My dear fellow," said Henri, who rarely passed up an opportunity for irony, "since like everyone else you may one day need discretion, and since I'm very fond of you . . . Yes, very fond! On my word of honor, if you needed a thousand franc note to stop you from blowing your brains out, you'd find it here, for we have no mortgage, have we Paul? If you were fighting a duel tomorrow, I'd measure the distance and load the pistols so that you might be killed by the rules. And if someone other than myself took it into his head to slander you behind your back, he would have to reckon with the rough gentleman who lives in my skin—that's what I call a friendship for all seasons. Ah well, when you find you're in need of discretion, my boy, remember: There are two kinds of discretion, one active and one passive. Passive discretion is the sort practiced by fools who use silence, denial, sullenness, the discretion of closed doors— mere impotence! Active discretion proceeds by assertion. If this evening at the club I were to say: 'Honest to God, the *girl with the golden eyes* was not worth what she cost me!' everyone, when I'd left, would exclaim: 'Did you hear that fop de Marsay, trying to convince us he's already had the *girl with the golden eyes?* He's no fool. He'd like to discourage his rivals.' But a trick like this is vulgar and dangerous. We might blather the silliest nonsense, there's always some idiot prepared to believe it. The best discretion is the kind used by clever wives who want to fool their husbands. It consists of compromising a woman we're not attached to, or one we don't love or haven't possessed, to save the honor of the woman we love enough to respect. That is what I call *the screen-woman.* Ah! Here's Laurent. What have you got for us?"

"Ostende oysters, Monsieur le Comte . . ."

"One day, Paul, you will know how entertaining it is to trifle with society while concealing the secret of your affections. I take tremendous pleasure in eluding the idiotic jurisdiction of the mass of men who never know what they want or what they're being made to want, who mistake the means for the end and alternately deify and damn, exalt and destroy! What a pleasure it is to foist emotions on them but accept none, to control but never obey! If there's anything to be proud of, isn't it a power we've acquired ourselves and of which we are both cause and effect, principle and result? Ah well, no man knows who I love or what I want. Perhaps they might know who I've loved, what I've loved, what I've wanted, as one knows the conclusion to a drama. But showing them my hand—that would be weakness, gullibility. I know nothing more contemptible than force outflanked by cunning. I'm becoming an amused initiate in the calling of ambassador, if only diplomacy were as difficult as life! Which I doubt. Are you ambitious? Do you want to make something of yourself?"

"Henri, you're making fun of me, as if I were not mediocre enough to do anything."

"Fine, Paul! If you go on laughing at yourself, you'll soon be able to laugh at everyone."

After lunch, while smoking his cigars, de Marsay began to take a singular view of the events of the previous night. Like many great minds, his insight was not spontaneous, and he could not instantly get to the bottom of things. Like all gifted natures with the capacity to live fully in the present—to suck the marrow from it, as it were, and devour it—his second thoughts needed a night's sleep to identify causes. Cardinal Richelieu had a mind like this, which did not prevent him from having the gift of foresight needed for the conception of great things. De Marsay was similarly gifted in all respects, but at first he used his weapons only to advance his pleasures; and only when he was sated with the pleasures that have pride of place in a wealthy and powerful young man's thoughts did he become one of the shrewdest politicians of his time. In this way a man hardens his heart: He uses women so that women cannot use him.

De Marsay realized, then, that the *girl with the golden eyes* had toyed with him; he was able to put the previous night in perspective, which had begun with a slow trickle of pleasures and ended in overflowing torrents. Now he could read this page glittering with superficial effects and find its hidden meaning. Paquita's purely physical innocence, her astonished joy, a few words that had escaped in the midst of her pleasure, obscure at first but now quite clear, convinced him that he had been standing in for someone else. Since he was familiar with corrupt social practices and perfectly indifferent to all forms of moral caprice, justifying such caprices by the satisfaction they provide, he was not shocked by vice and knew it as intimately as an old friend; but he was offended at the thought of serving as its fodder. If his presumptions were correct, he had been outraged to the very core of his being. This mere suspicion put him in a fury, and he roared like a tiger teased by a gazelle, the fury of a tiger that combined a beast's strength with the intelligence of a demon.

"Well, what's wrong, then?" Paul said to him.

"Nothing!"

"If someone asked you whether you had something against me and you answered with a *nothing* like that, we would probably fight a duel the next day."

"I no longer duel," de Marsay said.

"That seems even more tragic. Do you simply murder then?"

"You're twisting words. I execute."

"My dear friend," Paul said, "your jokes run toward black humor this morning."

"What do you expect? Lust leads to ferocity. Why? I haven't any idea, and I have no curiosity to find out. These cigars are excellent. Pour your friend some tea. Do you know, Paul, that I lead a pointless life? It's high time to choose a goal, to devote my powers to something that makes life worth living. Life is an odd comedy. I'm afraid I laugh at the triviality of our social order. The government cuts the heads off poor devils who've killed a man, and certifies creatures who, medically speaking, dispatch a dozen young people every winter. Morality is helpless against a dozen vices that are destroying society but cannot be punished. Another cup? Upon my honor, man is a clown dancing on the edge of a cliff. We're told about the immorality of *Les Liaisons dangereuses*, and some book with the name of a chamber maid. But there is one ghastly, dirty, dreadful, corrupting book that is always open and never closed, the great book of the world—not to mention another book, a thousand times more dangerous, that consists of everything passed on by word of mouth between men or women behind their fans at the ball."

"Henri, surely something extraordinary has happened to you, and that is obvious despite your active discretion."

"True. But listen, I have time to kill before this evening. Let's go gambling. Perhaps I'll be lucky enough to lose."

De Marsay rose, took a handful of bank notes, rolled them up in his cigar case, dressed, and took advantage of Paul's carriage to go to the Salon des Etrangers, where he spent the time until dinner in those thrilling bouts of winning and losing that are the last resource of strong constitutions when they are forced to operate in a vacuum. He came to the rendezvous at the appointed time that evening, and calmly allowed himself to be blindfolded. Then, with the firm resolve that only powerful men have the capacity to muster, he concentrated and applied his intelligence to guessing the route of the carriage. He was certain he was being taken down Rue Saint-Lazare and to the garden gate of the San-Réal mansion. When he passed through this gate, as he had done the first time, and was put on a stretcher borne most likely by the mulatto and the coachman, he understood, as he heard the sand crunch beneath their feet, why they were taking such scrupulous precautions. Had he been free or on foot, he might have broken off a twig from a shrub, or examined the sand sticking to his boots; whereas, transported by air, so to speak, into an otherwise inaccessible mansion, his great adventure must remain what it had been until then: a dream.

But man, to his despair, is imperfect in all he does, whether good or evil. All his intellectual or physical works are marked by the stamp of destruction. There had been a light rain and the ground was damp. During the night the odors of vegetation are much stronger than during the day; Henri inhaled the scent of mignonette along the path by which he was conveyed. This detail would help him in the investigations he vowed to make to discover the mansion that contained Paquita's boudoir. In the same fashion he studied his bearers' detours inside the house, and thought he would be able to recall them.

As on the previous evening, he found himself on the divan before Paquita, who undid his scarf; but he saw her pale and changed. She had been weeping. Kneeling like an angel at prayer, but a sad and deeply melancholy angel, the poor girl no longer resembled the curious, impatient, bounding creature who had taken de Marsay on her wings and transported him to the seventh heaven of love. There was something so real in this despair veiled by sensuality that the vengeful de Marsay felt an admiration for this new masterpiece of nature, and forgot for a moment the chief purpose of his visit.

"What's the matter, my Paquita?"

"Dear friend," she said, "take me away this very night! Cast me someplace where no one can say, 'There is Paquita', and no one can reply: 'There is a girl here with golden eyes and long hair.' There I will ply you with the pleasures of love as long as you want me. And when you no longer love me, you will leave me, and I shall not utter a word of complaint. You must feel no remorse, for one day spent with you, a single day looking at you will be worth a whole lifetime. But if I stay here, I am lost."

"I cannot leave Paris, my child," Henri answered. "I'm not a free agent; I'm bound by oath to several people who are bound to me in return. But I can find you a refuge in Paris where no human power can reach you."

"No," she said, "you're forgetting the power of the feminine."

Never had a sentence uttered by a human voice expressed such absolute terror.

"What harm can come to you if I interpose myself between you and the world?"

"Poison!" she said. "Doña Concha already suspects you. And," she continued, letting the bright tears run down her cheeks, "it's easy to see that I've changed. Well, if you abandon me to the fury of the monster who will devour me, let your sacred will be done! But come, let all life's pleasures be fulfilled in our love. Besides, I'll beg, I'll weep, I'll shout, I'll defend myself, perhaps I'll even manage to escape."

"Who will you implore this way?" he said.

"Silence!" Paquita went on. "If I'm granted salvation, it will perhaps be thanks to my discretion."

"Give me my dress then," said Henri cunningly.

"No, no," she vehemently replied, "stay as you are, one of those angels they taught me to hate, whom I looked upon only as monsters, while you are the loveliest creature under heaven," she said, caressing Henri's hair. "You don't know what an idiot I am. I've learned nothing. Since the age of twelve I've been shut away from everyone. I don't know how to read or write, and I speak only English or Spanish."

"How is it, then, that you receive letters from London?"

"My letters! Look, here they are!" she said, taking some papers from a tall Japanese vase.

She handed the letters to de Marsay, and the young man was surprised to see strange figures like those of a rebus traced in blood, expressing the most passionate feelings.

"But," he cried, admiring these hieroglyphs created by a cunning jealousy, "are you in the power of some evil genius?"

"Evil," she repeated.

"But how did you manage to go out . . ."

"Ha!" she said, "that was my downfall. I gave Doña Concha the choice between instant death and future anger. I had a demonic curiosity, I wanted to break out of this bronze ring they've drawn between me and creation, I wanted to see what young men were like, for the only men I know are the Marquis and Christemio. Our coachman and the valet are old men . . ."

"But surely you were not always shut away? Your health would suffer . . ."

"Ah!" she replied, "we walked, but always at night and in the country, along the Seine, far from the crowds."

"Are you not proud to be loved this way?"

"No," she said, "no longer! Full as it is, this hidden life is nothing but darkness compared to light."

"What do you mean by light?"

"You, my handsome Adolphe! You, for whom I would give my life. All the passionate things I was told and that I inspired, I feel for you! For a certain time I understood nothing of existence, but now I know what it is to love. Until now I was only loved, but I did not love. I would leave everything for you—take me away. Take me as a plaything, if you like, but let me be near you until you break me."

"Will you have no regrets?"

"Not a single one!" she said, letting him read it in her eyes with their pure, clear tint of gold.

Am I the favorite, then? Henri wondered to himself. He suspected the truth, but he was disposed to forgive the offense in favor of such a naive love. I shall soon see, he thought.

While Paquita was not accountable to him for her past, her least memory struck him as criminal. So he had the strength of mind to think about her, to judge his mistress, and to study her behavior even as he surrendered to the most arousing pleasures that ever a fairy descended from the heavens had devised for her beloved. Paquita seemed to have been made for love by a doting nature. From one night to the next her feminine genius had made the swiftest progress. Whatever this young man's power and his nonchalance in the realm of pleasure, despite his sated state the previous evening, he found in the *girl with the golden eyes* that seraglio the loving woman knows how to create and which a man can never refuse. Paquita responded to the passion that all truly great men feel for the infinite, a mysterious passion so dramatically expressed in *Faust*, so poetically translated in *Manfred*, and the passion for which so many pursuers of phantoms have searched, which scholars believe they glimpse in science and mystics find in God alone. De Marsay was ravished by the hope of possessing at last the ideal being with whom there would be constant struggle but no fatigue, and for the first time in many years, he opened his heart. His nerves relaxed, his coldness melted in the heat of this burning soul, his cynicism vanished, and happiness colored his existence white and rose, like the boudoir. Spurred on by a superior sensuality, he was transported beyond the limits of what he had hitherto defined as passion. He did not want to be outdone by this girl, whom a sort of artificial love had shaped in advance to meet the needs of his soul, and in the vanity that pushes man to dominate he found the strength to subdue this girl. Yet crossing over that line where the soul is mistress of itself, he lost himself in that delicious limbo which the vulgar so stupidly call *imaginary space*. He was tender; he was good; he was communicative. He drove Paquita nearly mad.

"Why shouldn't we go to Sorrento, Nice, Chiavari, and spend our whole life this way? Would you like that?" he said to Paquita in a penetrating voice.

"Do you really need to ask me '*Would you like that?*'" she cried. "Have I any will? I exist outside you only to give you pleasure. If you want to choose a retreat worthy of us, Asia is the only land where love can spread its wings . . ."

"You're right," Henri replied. "Let's go to the Indies—where spring is eternal, where the earth is full of flowers, where a man can live like a king without provoking gossip, as he does in the foolish lands where they try to realize the dull illusion of equality. Let us go to the country where one lives amid a race of slaves, where the sun is always shining on a white palace, where perfumes fill the air, where the birds sing of love, and where one dies when one can no longer love . . ."

"And where we shall die together!" said Paquita. "But let's not wait until tomorrow, let's go now and take Christemio."

"I swear, the most beautiful conclusion to life is pleasure. Yes, let's go to Asia. But leaving, child, takes a great deal of gold, and to have gold one must put one's affairs in order."

She understood nothing of such matters.

"There's plenty of gold here, as high as that!" she said, raising her hand.

"But it's not mine."

"What's the difference?" she replied, "if we need it, let's take it."

"It doesn't belong to you."

"Belong!" she repeated. "Haven't you taken me? When we have taken it, it will belong to us."

He began to laugh.

"Poor innocent creature! You know nothing about the things of this world."

"No, but this is what I do know," she cried, drawing Henri to her.

Just as he began to forget his suspicions and think only of possessing this creature forever, de Marsay felt a dagger thrust in the midst of his joy that ripped through his heart; and for the first time he was mortified. Paquita, who had raised him vigorously above her as if to gaze at him, had cried out: "Oh, Mariquita!"

"Mariquita!" roared the young man, "now I know everything I tried not to believe."

He leaped to the chest where the long dagger was kept. Fortunately for her and for him, it was locked. This obstacle only fueled his rage. But he recovered his self-control, took his cravat, and approached her with such furious purpose that, without knowing what crime she had committed, Paquita understood she was about to die. So in a single bound she leaped to the other end of the room to avoid the fatal knot de Marsay was about to tie around her neck. A struggle ensued. They were equally supple, agile, and vigorous. To end the struggle, Paquita tripped her lover by throwing a cushion at his legs, and she took advantage of this momentary respite to push the button that sounded an alarm. The mulatto quickly arrived. In the blink of an eye Christemio leaped on de Marsay, pinned him to the ground, put his foot on his chest and his heel to his throat. De Marsay realized that if he kept struggling he would be crushed at the least sign from Paquita.

"Why did you want to kill me, my love?" she asked him.

De Marsay did not reply.

"How have I displeased you?" she said to him. "Speak, let us understand each other."

Henri maintained the phlegmatic attitude of a strong man who knows he's been beaten: He preserved a cold, silent, very English demeanor, a momentary resignation that revealed a consciousness of his dignity. Besides, it had already occurred to him, despite his transport of anger, that it was hardly prudent to compromise himself legally by killing this girl on impulse, without carefully planning the murder to ensure his impunity.

"My beloved," Paquita continued, "speak to me. Don't leave me without a loving farewell! I wouldn't want to remember only the fright you've just given me. Will you speak?" she said, stamping her foot with anger.

In reply de Marsay shot her a look that so clearly meant *You will die!* that Paquita rushed toward him.

"Oh yes, you want to kill me? If my death can give you pleasure, kill me!"

She made a sign to Christemio, who lifted his foot off the young man and stepped away without any facial expression revealing a judgment on Paquita, good or bad.

"Now there's a man!" said de Marsay, solemnly gesturing toward the mulatto. "There is nothing like the devotion of friendship that suspends judgment. You have a true friend in this man."

"I'll give him to you if you like," she replied. "If I order him to do so, he'll serve you with the same devotion he's had for me."

She expected some reply, and continued in a voice full of tenderness: "Adolphe, speak to me kindly. It will soon be daybreak."

Henri did not answer. This young man had one unfortunate quality, for we tend to regard everything that seems powerful as great, and men often deify what is extravagant. Henri did not know how to forgive. The capacity to revise past judgments, which is certainly one of the graces of the soul, was meaningless to him. The ferocity of men of the North that strongly taints English blood had been passed on to him by his father. He was unshakable in both his positive and his negative feelings. Paquita's exclamation was all the more dreadful to him as it had hurled him down from the sweetest triumph that had ever inflated his male vanity. Hope, love, and all the other feelings that had been exalted in him had burned in his heart and mind; then these flames, ignited to illuminate his life, had been snuffed out by a cold wind. Paquita, stupefied and wretched, could barely summon the strength to give the signal for departure.

"This is useless," she said, throwing away the blindfold. "If he no longer loves me, if he hates me, it's all over."

She waited for him to look at her, he did not, and she fell back half dead. The mulatto shot Henri such a dreadful look that for the first time in his life, this young man, known to be unusually intrepid, trembled with fear.

If you do not love her, if you do her the slightest harm, I will kill you—such was the meaning of that rapid glance. De Marsay was led with almost servile care the length of a corridor illuminated by ancient torches and out through a secret door in a hidden staircase that led to the garden of the San-Réal mansion. The mulatto made him walk carefully along a lane of linden trees ending at a little gate, which opened onto a deserted street. De Marsay observed everything; the carriage was waiting for him. This time the mulatto did not join him; and when Henri put his head to the window to catch a last glimpse of the house and gardens, he met the white eyes of Christemio, and they exchanged a look. This was a mutual provocation, a challenge, the declaration of guerrilla war, of a duel that dispensed with normal laws, in which treachery and betrayal were part of the game. Christemio knew that Henri had sworn Paquita's death. Henri knew that Christemio would try to kill him before he could kill Paquita. The two understood each other perfectly.

The plot thickens—how interesting, Henri said to himself.

"Where is the gentleman going?" the coachman asked him.

De Marsay had himself driven to Paul de Manerville's.

enri stayed away from home for more than a week, and during this time no one had any idea where he was or what he was doing. This retreat saved him from the mulatto's rage but sealed the doom of the poor creature who had pinned all her hopes on the man she loved as no creature had ever loved on this earth. On the last day of the week, toward eleven o'clock in the evening, Henri came by carriage to the garden gate of the San-Réal mansion. Three men accompanied him. The coachman was obviously a friend, for he held himself upright on his seat like an alert sentinel, listening for the slightest sound. One of the others was posted in the street just outside the gate. The third man, who held a ring of keys in his hand, accompanied de Marsay.

"Henri," he said to his companion, "we've been betrayed."

"By whom, my good Farragus?"

"They're not all asleep," the leader of the Devorants* replied. "Clearly someone in the house took no time to eat or drink. Look, there's a light."

"We have a floorplan of the house: Where is the light coming from?"

"I don't need a floorplan to know that," answered Ferragus; "it's coming from the Marquise's room."

"Ah!" cried de Marsay. "She must have arrived today from London. This woman will have already stolen my revenge! But if she's beaten me to it, my good Gratien, we'll turn her over to the law."

"Listen! The deed is done," said Ferragus to Henri. The two friends stopped to listen and heard muffled cries that would have softened even a tiger's heart.

"The Marquise did not imagine that sounds could escape through the chimney," said the leader of the Devorants, with the laughter of a critic delighted to discover a defect in an otherwise fine piece of work.

"We alone know how to anticipate everything," Henri said. "Wait for me, I want to see what's going on up there, to find out how they settle their family squabbles. Good God, I think she's roasting her over a slow fire."

De Marsay climbed nimbly up the familiar stairs and recognized the way to the boudoir. When he

---

*The Companions of Duty, the secret society of the Thirteen.

opened the door, he gave an involuntary shudder, which the sight of bloodshed provokes in even the most ruthless man, and the spectacle that met his gaze gave him further cause for astonishment. The Marquise was a woman, after all, and she had contrived her vengeance with the treacherous perfection typical of the weaker animals. She had dissembled her anger in order to be sure of the crime before she punished it.

"Too late, my beloved!" said the dying Paquita, turning her pale eyes toward de Marsay.

The *girl with the golden eyes* lay dying in a pool of blood. All the blazing sconces, the delicate perfume that filled the air, a certain disorder in which the eye of an experienced man would have detected the mad abandon common to all passions, announced that the Marquise had shrewdly interrogated the guilty girl. This white room, in which blood seemed so decorative, gave evidence of a protracted struggle. Paquita's hands were imprinted on the cushions. In every corner she had clung to life, she had defended herself, and she had been stabbed. Whole shreds of fluted hangings were torn by her bloody hands, which surely fought long and hard. Paquita must have tried to scale the walls. Marks had been left by her naked feet as she tried to run along the back of the divan. Her body, stabbed repeatedly by her executioner's dagger, eloquently revealed how fiercely she had fought for a life that Henri had made dear to her. She was lying on the floor, and as she was dying she had bitten through the muscles of Madame de San-Réal's instep. The Marquise was still holding the bloody dagger in her hand, and her hair had been pulled; she was covered with bleeding bites, and her torn dress revealed her half-naked body with its lacerated breasts. She was magnificent. Her furious head was avidly inhaling the scent of blood. Her panting mouth was half-open, her nostrils unable to draw sufficient breath. Certain enraged animals leap upon their enemy, make the kill, then instantly recover their calm as if they've forgotten everything. Others stalk around their victim, guarding it for fear that another will snatch it from them, and, like Homer's Achilles, drag their enemy by the feet nine times around the walls of Troy. This was the Marquise. She did not see Henri at first, she was too certain of being alone to fear witnesses. Then, she was too intoxicated by warm blood, too stimulated by the struggle, in too great a state of exaltation to have noticed had all of Paris formed a circle around her. Lightning might have struck and it would not have registered. She had not even heard Paquita's last sigh, and thought the dead girl could still hear her.

"Die without confession!" she said to her. "Go to

hell, ungrateful monster; belong to no one but the devil. For the blood you've given him, you owe me all of yours! Die! Die a thousand deaths. I was too good, I took only a moment to kill you and I should have made you suffer all the pain you've beqeathed to me. But I have to live, to live miserably, with no one to love, now, but God!" She gazed at Paquita. "She's dead!" she said to herself after a pause, with a violent reversal of feeling. "Dead—oh, I shall die of sorrow!"

The Marquise was about to throw herself on the divan, stricken by a despair that took her breath away, when she finally caught sight of Henri de Marsay.

"Who are you?" she said to him, rushing toward him with the dagger raised.

Henri grabbed her arm, and so they could look at each other face to face. A ghastly surprise chilled the blood in both their veins, and they stood trembling like frightened horses. Indeed, twins could not have been more alike. Speaking at the same time, they asked: "Surely Lord Dudley is your father?"

And each one nodded in assent.

"She was faithful to the blood," Henri said, gesturing toward Paquita.

"She was as innocent as can be," replied Margarita-Euphémie Porraberil, who threw herself on Paquita's body with a cry of despair. "Poor girl! Oh, how I wish I could bring you back to life! I was wrong, forgive me, Paquita! You are dead, and I am alive! I am the unhappiest of women."

At this moment the terrible face of Paquita's mother appeared.

"You're going to tell me that you didn't sell her to me so that I might kill her," cried the Marquise. "I know why you've come from your lair. I'll pay you double for her. Keep quiet now."

She took a sack of gold from the ebony table and threw it disdainfully at the old woman's feet. The ring of gold had the power to bring a smile to the impassive features of the Georgian woman.

"I've come just in time, my sister," Henri said. "The law is going to question you . . ."

"Never," answered the Marquise. "Only one person could call me to account for this girl. And Christemio is dead."

"And the mother?" asked Henri, indicating the old woman, "Won't she continue to blackmail you?"

"She comes from a country where women are not human beings but things; you can do as you like with them, buy them and sell them, kill them, use them to indulge your whims the way you do here with your furniture. Besides, she has one passion that overrules all others, and which would have annihilated her maternal love, if she had loved her daughter; a passion . . ."

"And what is that?" Henri asked urgently, interrupting his sister.

"Gambling, God protect you from it!" answered the Marquise.

"But who is going to help you eliminate the traces of this fantasy, which the law would not overlook?" Henri asked, looking at the *girl with the golden eyes*.

"I have her mother," the Marquise replied, indicating the old Georgian, signaling her to stay.

"We will meet again," said Henri, who was anxiously thinking of his friends and feeling the need to leave.

"No, my brother," she said, "we will never meet again. I shall return to Spain to enter the convent of *Los Dolores*."

"You are still too young and beautiful," said Henri, taking her in his arms and kissing her.

"Good-bye," she said. "Nothing can console us for losing our idea of the infinite."

Eight days later, Paul de Manerville met de Marsay at the Tuileries, on the terrace of Feuillant's.

"Well now, you rascal, what has become of our beautiful girl with the golden eyes?"

"She died."

"Of what?"

"A chest complaint."